"Why are you here?" Sean asked.

Kate took a sip of strong tea before answering. "I wanted to see my nephew, of course."

"If that were all of it, you'd have been here a long time before now."

"I guess you could say I'm looking for myself," she replied. She gazed straight into his eyes. "You were the one who said I needed a life of my own."

Sean poured tea into the second cup and sat down across from her. "Are you serious about that?"

"I turned thirty a few days ago, Sean, and look at me. I've never been married, never borne a child, never even worked at a real job that I landed on my own."

"And now you're out for adventure?" he asked.

"Something like that."

Even in the firelight, Kate could see the mischief dancing in his eyes. "Well, I think I can certainly provide you with one of those."

LINDA LAEL MILLER

JUST KATE

MIRA BOOKS

ISBN 1-55166-055-5

JUST KATE

Copyright © 1989 by Linda Lael Miller.

Printed in U.S.A.

For my all-weather friends,
Susan Crose and Nancy Bush,
first on the scene
with an umbrella when it rains,
clapping for joy when the sun shines

1

The exchange was so blatant, so audacious that Kate Blake couldn't believe she'd seen it. The lobby was crowded, and people swirled past her, laughing and talking as they waited for the opera to resume. Kate stood frozen in their midst, fingers curved around her glass of intermission orange juice, her indigo eyes wide, afraid even to blink.

She hadn't imagined it. Brad had handed another man a packet of white powder and taken money in return, right there in front of half the population of Seattle.

Perhaps, she thought desperately, it was all a mistake. Perhaps she had only imagined that the packet contained cocaine, and that Brad, the man she'd meant to marry in less than a month, had just accepted money for it.

In the next instant, Brad turned, tucking a folded bill into the pocket of his coat as he moved. His eyes met Kate's, and it was clear that he knew she'd seen. There was no apology in his gaze, however, only defiance. Then he was looking at his companion again, and Kate might not have existed at all.

She felt dizzy, and then claustrophobic, and she knew she had to get out into the fresh air fast. She set her cup aside and hurried toward the main door.

Outside, Kate gripped the stair railings in both hands and dragged in deep, clean breaths until the choking sensation passed. A glance back over one elegantly bared shoulder told her that Brad hadn't followed. He probably hadn't even noticed she was gone.

She looked up at the dark, star-speckled sky aglow with city lights, and her vision blurred as tears filled her eyes. She was torn. One part of her wanted to go back inside, grip Brad by the lapels and demand to know why he'd thrown everything away; another preferred to pretend that nothing had changed.

Kate inched down the stairs, still grasping the railing with both hands. Brad was the man she'd planned to marry. He was her father's campaign manager. And she'd just seen him break the law in the most brazen of ways.

A thousand thoughts whirled through her head. This wasn't new behavior for Brad; she was certain of that. And yet she hadn't known. She'd been engaged to him and *she hadn't known* what kind of man he was! How could that be?

There were no cabs lined up in front of the theater, since the opera would run another full hour. Kate looked back again, knowing she should go inside, call for a taxi and wait in the lobby until it arrived. But something within her demanded action. She needed to walk, hard and fast, with the cool, clean night wind blowing against her face. She started out in the general direction of her downtown condominium, chin held high, her grandmother's antique brass evening bag swinging at her side.

Hard-eyed street people watched her pass, but there was none of the usual panhandling. Kate supposed that in her present mood she didn't look approachable.

Moments later, as she passed a popular department store, her pace slackened. The breeze had dried her tears. Kate's reflection in the windows regarded her forlornly as she took in her own tall, slender body, the sleek designer gown that had cost the earth, the soft, Gibson-girl arrangement of her dark hair.

"So who wanted to marry Bradley Wilshire anyway?" she demanded aloud. As she rounded the corner, Kate was careful not to look at her image in the glass, fearing it might answer, *You did.*

Kate pulled her paisley silk shawl around her bare shoulders and shivered. In just a few minutes, she reminded herself, she would be home in her small, elegant condominium overlooking the harbor. She would put classical music on the stereo, pour herself a glass of low-cal Chablis and spend the rest of the evening soaking in a bubble bath.

Was it possible that Brad was a pusher?

Trying to forget what she'd seen would be useless, she knew, but the ramifications were more than she could deal with, too big to take in all at once.

She was nearly home, just passing the Commercial Bank building, when she noticed two men standing in front of the cash machine. Kate considered crossing to the other side of the street, but they seemed so engrossed in conversation that they probably wouldn't notice her, anyway.

The man facing Kate was tall and well built, familiar in a disturbing sort of way. In the dim light of the cash machine, she could see he was wearing a tuxedo, and his mouth was curved into an ingenuous smile. She sensed he was aware of her presence, though he gave no sign of it.

"Take it easy now, mate," he said in a thick Australian accent. "If it's money you want, you'll have it, but the machine will only give me so much in a twenty-four hour period."

An almost dizzying sensation of mingled despair and excitement filled Kate. The voice, the accent—it couldn't be!

It was then that Kate spotted the glint of a switchblade in the second man's hand.

She was filled with instant ire. Thanks to Brad, she'd seen her share of crime for the day, and she was fed up. Without considering possible results, she spun her grandmother's purse on its chain until it became a whistling blur. When it struck the mugger in the side of the head, he dropped the knife. In the same instant, his knees folded and he sank to the sidewalk in an unlikely position of prayer.

The tall man collected the knife, recessed the blade with an unsettling expertise and tucked it into his pocket. "Nice work, Katie," he said, reclaiming a gold credit card from the slot on the cash machine, "but you shouldn't have taken a chance like that. The bleeder might have turned on you."

Kate sank against the rough concrete wall of the bank, not trusting her knees to support her. "Sean," she whispered.

His white teeth flashed in the night. The mugger started to rise from the sidewalk, but his would-be victim pushed him back down with a light, deft touch of one foot.

Kate thought she was going to be sick and put one hand to her mouth.

"Surprised to see me, are you?" Sean asked.

Kate lowered her hand. Holding her knees rigid and her backbone straight, she started to walk away. "I'll call the police," she said woodenly.

Sean stopped her by taking a light but inescapable hold on her elbow. "No need of that, love," he said in a gravelly tone that made sweet chills ripple over Kate's soul. "They're here already."

Kate glanced toward the street. Sure enough, a black-and-white was pulling up to the curb. She considered having herself taken into protective custody until Sean Harris had gone back to Australia, where he undeniably belonged.

"What's going on here?" asked the older of two officers.

Sean explained, and the moaning mugger was hauled unceremoniously to his feet. Kate listened numbly as his rights were read, her teeth sinking into her lower lip. Sean's grasp on her arm never slackened.

"You and the lady will need to come to the station and swear out a complaint," said the younger officer.

"And if we don't?" Sean asked, arching one dark eyebrow.

"They'll have to let him go," Kate answered.

"Can't have that," Sean replied lightly. "My car's just up the street—we'll follow you."

Both policemen touched the brims of their hats in a deferential fashion before hustling the prisoner into the back of the squad car. Sean fairly hurled Kate into the passenger seat of a late-model sports car parked half a block away.

"Well," he said, when they were following the police, "fancy meeting you here, Katie-did."

Kate folded her arms. First Brad's drug deal, then the mugging and now this. Boy, had her horoscope been off target this morning. "My parents would have appreciated a telephone call," she said stiffly, doing her best to ignore her former brother-in-law. "They worry about Gil, you know."

The reference to his young son did not visibly move Sean. At least Kate didn't catch him reacting, though she was watching him out of the corner of her eye.

"They know where we live," he replied, and this time his voice was as cold as a Blue Mountain snowfall.

Kate unfolded her arms and tried to relax. It was almost incomprehensibly bad luck that, of all the muggings she might have stumbled upon, it had to be Sean's. She hadn't seen him since Abby's funeral, and she'd hoped that she would never lay eyes on him again.

She drew in a deep breath and let it out again slowly. "Did you bring Gil with you?" she asked.

"Now why would I drag the poor little nipper from one hemisphere to the other like that?" he countered.

Kate suppressed an urge to wind up her purse again and let Sean have it. "Maybe because his grandparents would like to see him," she said.

"Because they'd like to take him away, you mean," Sean answered, "and turn him into a proper little Yank."

"He's half-American," Kate pointed out, daring at last to turn in the car seat and look directly at Sean. His profile was rugged, like the outback he loved so much. "What's wrong with that?"

They had reached the police station, and Sean was spared having to answer—for the moment.

The next hour was consumed by the dubious process of pressing charges against the mugger. Kate seriously considered turning Brad in for pushing drugs while she was there, but she knew she couldn't do that without consulting her father. An unforeseen scandal might ruin his chances for reelection to the Senate; Kate had to give him time to prepare.

She went to the telephone when she was through issuing her statement and dialed the familiar number.

Her mother answered; it was late enough that the staff was off duty. "Blake residence."

Kate braced herself. "Mother, it's Kate. I'm at the police station and—"

"The police station!" The horror in Irene Blake's voice was unmistakable. "Good heavens, what's happened? She's at the *police station*, dear!"

At this, the senator himself came on the line. Kate winced, just as if she'd been there to see him wrench the receiver out of her mother's hand. "What's this business about the police? So help me, Katherine, if you've been arrested, I'll fire you in an instant."

Kate made an effort to control her temper. "Of course I haven't been arrested, Daddy," she whispered into the phone, embarrassed. "I happened to witness a mugging, that's all."

"Are you all right?" the senator boomed. Now that he knew his career was safe, he could afford to be concerned about his daughter. Kate had never had any illusions about his priorities.

"I'm fine," she answered. "Daddy, the reason I'm calling is that—well—I ran into Sean."

"Sean who?" demanded the senator.

Kate felt a sweet, shivery sensation from head to foot, and looking to one side, she found that the handsome Australian was standing mere inches away. She reminded herself that he'd been Abby's husband, that he was a liar and a womanizer, but the tremulous, taut-bow feeling didn't subside. "Sean Harris," she finally managed to reply, her cheeks burning.

Sean's green eyes danced as he watched her color rise. Apparently he heard her father's question, for he took the receiver from Kate and spoke into it, his tone flippant and cool. "You know, Senator. That no-gooder from down under—the one that married your elder daughter."

Kate squeezed her eyes shut as she heard a burst of profanity explode on her father's end of the line. After a moment's recovery, she jerked the receiver out of Sean's hand and sputtered, "Daddy, remember your heart!"

The senator went right on swearing. He finally hung up with a crash, but not before blurting out a nonsensical sentence that ended in, "... bring that bastard here no matter what you have to do!"

Sean had heard that, too. He rocked back on his heels, his wonderful eyes full of laughter. "There's a welcome for you," he said.

Kate had a headache. She sighed and opened her purse, but there was no sign of the little metal box of aspirin she usually carried. All she found were her keys and a credit card. "He wants to talk to you about Gil," she said wearily. "That's all."

Sean didn't look at all convinced of that, but he offered Kate his arm and inclined his head to one side. "All right, Katie-did," he said, "I'll face the lion in his den. But I'm only doing it for you.''

Kate assessed this man who had caused her family so much heartache and shook her head. He didn't look the least bit remorseful to her.

"Thanks a whole heap," she said.

The lights of Seattle glittered and danced in the rearview mirror of Sean's car as he and Kate drove toward the Blake mansion. Even in the dim glow from the dashboard, she could see he was no longer amused. His jaw was set in a hard, ungiving line.

The confrontation between Sean and the senator would not be a pleasant experience for anyone.

Unexpectedly, Sean reached out and caught hold of Kate's left hand. His thumb pressed against the large diamond in Brad's engagement ring. "Who's the lucky man?" he asked. His tone was gruff, as though he was trying to be congenial and finding it difficult.

Kate's heart ached as she remembered the scene in the lobby at the opera house. She opened the lid of her antique purse, slid the ring off her finger and dropped it inside. "There isn't one," she said sadly. She was almost thirty years old, and her time for finding husbands and having babies was running out.

She felt rather than saw Sean's glance in her direction. "Funny. Abby always said you'd be the one to settle down and have a family."

He couldn't have known what pain that remark would foster—could he? Kate didn't know Sean Harris very well; it had been ten years since he'd married her sister in the garden behind the Blakes' house and five since Abby had driven her sports car off a cliff north of Sydney.

Kate's mother still believed Abby had died deliberately, unable to live with the unhappiness Sean caused her. Kate didn't know what to think.

She'd visited her sister in Australia several times, the last being when Gil was born seven years before. Although she'd watched Sean carefully, Kate hadn't seen any evidence of the emotional cruelty Abby had written home about. Oh, Sean might have been a little distant where Abby was concerned, but he'd been crazy about his infant son. Anyone could have seen that.

"Kate?"

The prompt from Sean brought her back to the present with a start. She pointed one finger. "Turn right on this next street."

Sean took a new hold on Kate's hand. "I remember," he said. "Katie, what happened?"

Kate lowered her eyes. "I thought I was in love," she confessed. "Tonight I saw Brad do something terrible."

He squeezed her hand. "You're better off out of it if you have any doubts at all," he said.

Kate had no doubt that was true, but she still wished she could go back in time and wave a wand and alter reality. In the new scenario Brad would only be making change for a twenty-dollar bill or giving someone his business card.

They had reached the foot of the Blakes' long brick-paved driveway, and the gates opened immediately. Of course, the senator had been watching for their arrival from inside the house, the gate controls in his hands.

"I don't know why I'm doing this," Sean muttered.

Kate sighed. "And my horoscope said I'd have a good day," she said as they passed through the gates.

"You don't believe in that rot, do you?" Sean asked, and he sounded short-tempered. He couldn't be blamed for dreading what was ahead, Kate supposed. She wasn't looking forward to it, either.

"Not anymore I don't," she answered.

Senator John Blake was standing on the front porch when they reached the house, his hands shoved into the pockets of his heavy terry cloth bathrobe. Even in slippers and pajamas, Kate marveled to herself, he looked imperious—every inch the powerful politician.

And he was powerful. Careers were made and broken on his say-so.

Sean shut off the headlights and the engine and got out of the car. He walked around to help Kate, but she'd pushed the door open before he reached her.

"Where is the boy?" the senator demanded. No hello. No "What brings you all the way to America?" It was clear enough that Sean wasn't welcome in his own right.

"He's in school in Sydney, where he belongs," Sean answered. He'd never been the slightest bit intimidated by the senator, and Kate suspected that was one of the reasons her father disliked him so intensely.

Senator Blake doubled one hand into a fist and pounded it into his palm. "Blast it all, Harris, that child belongs with his family!"

"I'm his family," Sean said quietly. Kate felt a certain admiration for his composure, even though she wanted her sister's son to visit the United States on a regular basis as much as her parents did.

Kate's mother, Irene, appeared in the massive double doorway behind the senator. "Let's not stand outside, making a public spectacle of ourselves," she scolded. "There may be reporters from those awful tabloids lurking in the shrubbery."

Despite everything, Kate had to smile at that. The tabloids didn't pick on dull men like her father. They fed on scandal.

Then her smile faded as she stepped into the light and warmth of her parents' house. Once word of Brad's profitable little sideline got out, there would be scandal aplenty.

"What are you doing here?" the senator demanded of Sean the moment they were all inside his study with the doors closed. He sounded for all the world as though he thought Sean should have had his permission before entering the country.

"I've been in Seattle for a week, if it's any of your business," Sean answered evenly. "My company is thinking of placing an order with Simmons Aircraft."

Kate saw the sudden interest in her father's face. Simmons Aircraft was one of the largest employers in the state, and the company was a pet concern of the senator's. "You're still with the airline, then?"

"You could say that," Sean replied. A forest of crystal decanters stood on the bar, and he helped himself to a snifter of brandy, lifting it once to the senator before raising it to his lips. "But you didn't have your daughter drag me up here so we could talk about Austra-Air, did you?"

Kate felt a flash of resentment. Sean made it sound as though her father orchestrated her every move.

"No," Senator Blake responded. "It's about my grandson."

Sean set the snifter aside, then brought a thin leather wallet from the inside pocket of his tuxedo jacket, opening it and extending it to his former father-in-law. Kate caught a glimpse of a handsome blond boy smiling up from a photograph.

It was no secret that Gil resembled his late mother, but surprise moved in the senator's aging face all the same—surprise and pain. "He's a fine-looking lad," the old man said in a strange, small voice. "Does he do well in school?"

"Mostly," Sean answered quietly. "He's got a weak spot when it comes to spelling and the like."

Mrs. Blake hovered close behind the senator's shoulder, peering hungrily at her grandson's picture. "Abby was the same way," she said.

The air in that large, gracious room suddenly seemed to be in short supply. Kate went to the window behind her father's desk and opened one side a little way.

"The boy has a right to know his mother's family," said the senator.

"A few years ago I might have agreed with that," Sean replied, pulling the photograph out from behind the plastic window in his wallet and extending it to Mrs. Blake.

"What changed your mind?" the senator wanted to know. It seemed to Kate that he was having trouble meeting Sean's gaze, but she was wrong, of course. Her father was virtually fearless.

"When a man's son is nearly kidnapped," Sean answered, "it tends to change his mind about a lot of things." He tucked his wallet back into his pocket and glanced at Kate once before telling his late wife's parents, "You're welcome to visit Gil anytime you want to, but I won't send him here. Not until he's old enough to take care of himself."

Kate was staring at Sean, hardly able to believe what she'd heard. Gil had nearly been kidnapped? That in itself was news to her, but it had actually seemed, for a moment there, as though Sean thought the senator might have been behind the attempt.

When Sean walked out of the study, Kate followed, partly because she didn't want to listen to another of her father's tirades and partly because she had to confront Sean. He couldn't go around accusing good people of a crime and then just turn and walk away!

Kate said a hasty goodbye to her mother and father and followed Sean outside.

"I assume you want a ride home," Sean said as he opened the car door on the driver's side. It was the first indication he'd given that he was aware of her presence.

Kate answered by getting into the car. "What the hell do you mean by implying that my father would abduct a child?" she demanded the moment Sean was behind the wheel.

He ground the key into the ignition, and the engine started with an angry roar. "He wouldn't try it personally, of course," he snapped. "He paid someone to steal my son off the playground."

"That's a lie!"

Sean stopped the car without warning and glared at Kate. "Is it?" he rasped. "The man the police picked up admitted everything—he said he was working for a powerful American politician, and I guessed the rest."

Kate felt the color drain from her face. "No," she whispered, stunned. Her father would never do a thing like that. He was honorable and good, the kind of man who belonged in a Norman Rockwell painting. "I don't believe you."

"Believe what you like, love," Sean sighed. "I don't really give a damn."

Kate stiffened in her seat. "If my father was guilty," she challenged, "why didn't you take your case to the press? That would have ruined his career."

Sean didn't look at her. He appeared to be concentrating on the road, and his strong hands were tense where they gripped the steering wheel. "I couldn't," he answered in a low voice. "I once loved a daughter of his, you see."

Kate sat back. This had been one hell of a day. "So now you're just going to fly back home and forget that Gil has a family here in the States?"

They had reached the bottom of the driveway. "Yes," he replied. "If you want to see him, you'll have to pay a visit to the land of Oz."

Kate remembered the nickname Australians had given their country from her sister's early letters. The later ones had been filled with anger and fear and a wild, keening kind of despair. "I might just do that," she said. It would be good to get away from what Brad had done, away from her father's campaign.

Sean gave her a quicksilver glance, one she nearly missed. "Really?"

"I'd need to get a visa," Kate told him. "But, with my father's connections, that shouldn't take long."

Kate couldn't tell whether Sean was pleased at the prospect of a visit from his former sister-in-law or not, since the car was too dark and he revealed nothing by his tone or his words. "Where do you live?"

She gave him the address of her building, and he nodded in recognition. It was near his hotel, he said.

"How long are you staying?" she asked as the expensive car slipped through the dark city streets.

He moved his powerful shoulders in a casual shrug. "Another few days, I suppose. I want to take the plane up at least once more before I make my recommendation."

Kate knew he was testing the airliner his company was considering buying from Simmons Aircraft. "Just how many planes are we talking about here?" she asked.

Sean favored her with a grin that might have been slightly contemptuous. She couldn't quite tell. "You're definitely your father's daughter," he said, and Kate felt as though she'd been roundly insulted. Her cheeks were throbbing with heat when Sean finally answered her question. "Roughly a dozen, give or take a plane. We're phasing out our old fleet."

A dozen airliners. A contract like that would mean prosperity for a good many of her father's constituents.

"What do you do, anyway?" Sean asked.

Again Kate felt vaguely indignant. "I work for the senator."

"I gathered that much," Sean retorted, bringing the car to a sleek stop in front of Kate's building. "Do you actually work, or do you just stand around agreeing with everything the old man says?"

Kate's color rose in anger, and she reached for the door handle, but Sean caught her hand in a swift grasp and held it prisoner. She trembled as he stroked the tender flesh on the inside of her wrist with the pad of his thumb.

"Cold?" he asked, knowing perfectly well she was practically boiling.

She gave a little cry when he tilted his head and melded his mouth to hers, but she made no move to resist him. The old attraction had returned to shame her.

2

Kate's telephone was ringing when she let herself into the elegant condominium. She made no effort to lift the receiver, knowing the answering machine would pick up the call.

She listened to her own voice giving a recorded greeting as she carefully folded her silk shawl and set it aside, along with her grandmother's purse. There was a little dent, she noticed with a frown, where the solid brass bag had struck the mugger's head.

Brad's voice filled the room. At least there was one good thing about this whole incident, and that was the fact that Brad's job would be hers now. She was qualified, and she had more seniority than anyone else on the staff. "Kate, I'm at home. Call me immediately!"

"Go to hell," Kate muttered, her arms folded across her chest. Even though the living room was warm, she suddenly felt chilled. She turned down the volume on the machine and, if Brad said anything more, she didn't hear him.

Her mind and senses were full of Sean. Her heart was still beating a little faster than usual, and her nipples felt taut beneath the thin fabric of her evening gown. She kept her arms folded over her breasts in an effort to hide her involuntary response, even though there was no one around to see.

Unlike her parents, Kate didn't keep pictures of Abby out in plain view, but she went to the shelf behind her couch and took down a thin leather-bound album. The names "Abby and Sean" were embossed on the cover in gold lettering, and Kate felt a lump thicken in her throat as she opened it to the first photograph.

It showed Abby sitting at her vanity table in her frilly room, her wedding gown a tumble of satin and lace and pearls. Kate saw herself, ten years younger and wearing a pink bridesmaid's dress. In the photograph she appeared to be pinning Abby's veil carefully into place, though in reality that task had fallen to a hairdresser.

With the tip of an index finger, Kate touched her sister's glowing, flawless face, her golden hair and wide brown eyes. *Abby*. The senator had called her his Christmas-tree angel.

Tears brimmed in Kate's eyes, and she closed the album and put it carefully back among the others. She couldn't think about Abby, not with Sean's kiss still burning on her mouth.

Kate kicked off her shoes and felt her feet sink deep into the plush pearl-gray carpet on the floor. With a sigh, she wandered into her bedroom and slipped out of the dress, her panty hose and underthings. A long, hot shower soothed her a little, though the pounding massage of the water made her more aware of her body than she wanted to be.

Clad in a striped silk nightshirt, her shoulder-length brown hair blown dry, Kate climbed into the brass bed that had once graced one of her grandmother's guest rooms and pulled the covers up to her chin.

She wouldn't think about Sean. It was that simple. She had a good mind; she could direct it to other matters.

However, it would not be directed. Against Kate's will, she remembered the first time she'd seen Sean Harris.

She'd been nineteen at the time, and he'd come to the house with Abby. Attracted by his good looks, his sense of humor and his lilting accent, Kate had fallen in love. Although he had never said or done anything to encourage her, Sean had always been kind, and Kate had gone on adoring him long after he'd become her brother-in-law.

Then those letters had started arriving from Abby. Sean was a chauvinist, she'd claimed. He hated her, delighted in humiliating her.

"Why didn't you leave him?" Kate asked in the darkness of her room. She squeezed her eyes shut as memories of the funeral invaded her mind, unwanted and painful.

Sean had brought Abby home to be buried in the family plot, though Gil, only two years old then, had remained behind in Australia. Sean's grief had loomed over him, like the dark shadow of something monstrous.

Even then she had loved him, though she wouldn't have admitted that to herself. The guilt, coupled with her bereavement, would have broken her.

For the past five years Kate had concentrated on putting Sean out of her mind. Until tonight she'd thought those treacherous, tearing emotions were behind her forever.

Now she just didn't know.

A furious pounding at the front door awakened Kate with a start. She squinted at the clock on her bedside table and saw that it was two-thirty in the morning.

Full of frightened bafflement, Kate scrambled out of bed and found her robe. Reaching the front door, she peered through the peephole and saw Brad.

"Let me in, damn it," he snapped, somehow knowing she was there.

Kate hesitated, then opened the door. Brad was capable of making a scene, and there was no sense in letting him awaken all the neighbors.

The tall blond man pushed past Kate. He'd exchanged his formal evening clothes for a pair of corduroy slacks, a lightweight blue sweater and the formidably expensive leather jacket Kate had given him for Christmas.

"Why the devil did you run off like that?" he rasped, his eyes snapping with barely suppressed fury.

Kate bit her lower lip and brushed her sleep-tangled hair back from her face. He was referring to her hasty exit from the opera, of course. "I saw you take money for cocaine," she said slowly and carefully. Even now she could hardly believe it.

She hoped for a raging denial, but Brad only stared at her in hostile puzzlement. "So?" he asked.

Kate felt fury flow through her like venom. "What do you mean, 'So?'" she cried, struggling to keep her voice down. "We're talking about a crime here—a felony!"

Brad shook his handsome head in apparent amazement. "I don't believe this," he said.

"Neither do I," Kate replied wearily. She found her antique purse, opened it and took out the ring. "Here," she said, extending it to Brad.

His eyes widened in his tanned face. "You're not serious."

"I can't marry you," Kate said. Tears filled her eyes as she mourned all her dreams—the suburban house, the children, the dog in the back of a station wagon. All of it was gone. It wasn't fair.

Brad refused to take the ring. "Kate," he said reasonably as though speaking to a cranky child, "*everybody* does cocaine."

Kate shook her head. Her cheeks were wet now, and she dried them hastily on the sleeve of her nightshirt. "No," she argued. "That isn't true and you know it. Brad, you need help. If you'll check into a hospital—"

He held up both hands in a gesture so abrupt that it startled Kate into retreating another step. "Wait a second. A hospital? I haven't got that kind of problem, Kate. And even if I did, I wouldn't just walk away from the senator's campaign."

Kate swallowed. "You'll have to resign as campaign manager, Brad. Right away."

He was staring at her as though she'd just told him she'd had supper with a Martian. "Resign? Are you kidding? This is the most important job of my career and you damn well know it!"

Kate did know that Brad had political ambitions of his own. He had left a prestigious law firm to take the job on her father's staff expressly to make contacts among the powerful. "Brad, if you don't resign, my father will fire you."

Brad paled beneath his tan. "Are you saying that you're going to tell him about tonight?"

"I have to," Kate said with miserable conviction. "It would be irresponsible not to."

Brad stood close, his hands cupping Kate's face. Although his touch was gentle, she sensed a certain restrained violence in him and she was afraid. "No. Listen to me. You can't do this— I've worked too long and too hard . . ."

Kate twisted out of his grasp and put the pastel couch between them, her hands gripping its nubby back. "Go home," she said quietly. "Think about this. We'll talk again tomorrow."

"We'll talk now!" Brad snapped. "If you tell your father about that cocaine, I'll be ruined!"

"Please leave," Kate said. She felt chilled from head to foot. She had almost married this man!

Brad didn't move at all. He only glared at her and spit out, "You're naive as hell, Kate. This kind of thing goes on every day in every level of government. Why don't you stop being such a goody-goody and grow up?"

Kate could only gaze at him, feeling sick to her stomach. Dear God in heaven, how had he fooled her so completely?

After another long and frightening moment, Brad stormed out the door. Kate rushed to lock and bolt it behind him, leaning against it with her eyes closed while she waited for her heartbeat and her breathing to settle into normal patterns.

She'd been dating Brad Wilshire for a year. There must have been signs that he used and sold drugs, but she hadn't seen them. That fact in itself was terrifying; Kate wondered if she could trust her own instincts. Was she one of those self-destructive women she'd read about in pop psychology books?

After a few deep breaths and fifteen minutes spent pacing the darkened living room, Kate was tired enough to sleep. She crawled back into bed, closed her eyes and dreamed that she lived in a fine colonial house in the suburbs. Sean was her husband and Gil was her son and there were twelve gleaming airliners parked in the backyard.

The jangle of the telephone awakened Kate before her alarm clock could. She grappled for the receiver and pressed it to her ear, muttering a hoarse, "Hello?"

The senator's voice was like restrained thunder. "Brad has been arrested," he said.

Kate was wide awake. "When?" she asked, sitting up in bed.

"Early this morning. He's denying all the charges, of course."

Kate swallowed hard. "What charges?"

"You ought to know," her father responded coldly. "You're the one who turned him in, aren't you? How could you do this when you knew the effect a scandal would have on me?"

"I didn't turn him in," Kate protested quietly. "I would never have done that without consulting you."

"Be that as it may, the story will be all over the morning papers. We've got to decide whether to stand behind Wilshire or cut him loose."

"That shouldn't be too hard to work out," Kate said, flinging back the covers. "He's guilty—I saw him make the sale with my own eyes."

"But you didn't blow the whistle on him?"

"No," Kate insisted. "I should have, though."

"I take it the wedding is off?"

Kate shoved a hand through her hair. "I don't know how you can even ask that," she whispered furiously. "Of *course* it's off!"

The senator sighed. Kate knew he'd had dreams of his own where Brad was concerned. He'd meant to groom his prospective son-in-law to take his place one day. And John Blake wasn't a man who gave up easily. "I think I could persuade him to enter a treatment center."

"Give it up, Daddy," Kate sighed. "Brad will ruin you if you keep him on as campaign manager, and we both know it."

Her father reluctantly agreed and ended the conversation. Kate showered, wound her dark hair into a tidy French braid and dressed in a businesslike tweed suit and tasteful silk blouse. As her father's press secretary, she was ready to meet the newspaper reporters.

It was a good thing, because they were waiting for her the moment she reached the elegant mansion on the hill, clustering around her car, shouting questions and shoving microphones and cameras into her face.

"Is it true you turned your lover in for pushing cocaine?" called one man.

Kate looked at him with distaste and hustled toward the front door. "The senator will have a comment for you later," she called over one shoulder.

Someone grabbed her by the arm, and Kate wrenched free, infuriated by the presumption of such a gesture.

Inside the house she found her father surrounded by aides. There was no sign of her mother. Although Irene was a seasoned campaigner, she tended to get headaches when the water got rough.

"Are you ready to issue a statement?" Kate asked, shouldering her way through to her father's desk.

He looked up as though surprised to see her. "Yes," he said. "Tell those vultures out there that even though we bailed Wilshire out of jail, we're washing our hands of him as of today. He's off my staff."

"When will you name a new campaign manager?" Kate asked. She fully expected her father to give the job to her, since she'd earned it. In fact, in many ways she was more qualified than Brad had been.

"Right now," the senator said decisively. "Tell the press that I've chosen Mike Wilson for the job." He glanced fondly at the young and inexperienced lawyer standing close by.

Kate turned to leave the room without a word.

"Where do you think you're going?" Kate's father called after her, his tone angry and imperious.

Kate froze at the study door, her hand on the brass knob. "I'm about to issue my last official statement as your press secretary," she replied clearly.

The senator's anger was palpable. It reached out and coiled around Kate like an invisible boa constrictor. "Not until you've told me what this is all about, you won't!"

Kate turned and faced him again. "You as much as promised that job to me. How many times have you said, 'If it weren't for Brad, you'd be my campaign manager'?"

"I was only joking, and you damn well know it. It takes a man to manage a campaign! Furthermore, I don't have time to indulge your temperament, Katherine. If you walk out that door, you can consider yourself fired."

Kate glared at the white-haired man seated behind the desk. His staff surrounded him on three sides, all of them looking at Kate as though she'd just lost her reason.

She offered a silent prayer that she wouldn't cry and raised her chin. "That will save me the trouble of writing a letter of resignation," she said.

The senator swore, and Kate walked out of his study with her shoulders straight and her head high. Her mother was in the hallway, her perfect complexion gray with anxiety, her strawberry blond hair artfully coiffed. She gripped both of Kate's hands in hers, and her ice-blue eyes pleaded for understanding.

"I know your father is in a terrible mood," she said, "but it's sure to pass once the press backs off a little."

Kate could no longer hold back her tears. She shook her head and put one hand over her mouth.

"What's happened?" Irene Blake demanded.

Kate bit into her lower lip, struggling for composure. Her disappointment and sense of betrayal combined to overwhelm her. "He gave Brad's job to Mike Wilson," she finally managed to say.

Irene's gaze revealed honest bafflement. "And?"

Kate's patience was exhausted. "Mother, that job should have gone to me," she whispered angrily.

"But you're—"

"Don't you dare say 'But you're a woman,' Mother. If you do, I'll never forgive you."

Irene sighed. "Why don't you just go away for a few days, dear. Fly somewhere tropical and lounge in the sun until you feel better."

Kate sniffed and dried her cheeks with a tissue pulled from her purse. She still had to face the press. "That's a good idea, Mother. Tell Daddy I said, *adiós*, bye-bye and *ciao*." With that, she started toward the door.

"Don't be flippant, Katherine," her mother called after her. "It doesn't become you."

Kate rolled her eyes, opened the front door and stepped outside. Sean was just about to enter, and she couldn't have been happier to see him. He was like a barrier between her and the eager reporters. "Thank God you're here," she whispered.

Sean grinned, looking almost intolerably good in his jeans, cotton shirt and leather jacket. "Trust a Yank to do the unexpected," he said in a mischievous whisper that ruffled the loose tendrils of Kate's hair and sent a sweet shiver all through her system. "I was prepared to be thrown out on my ear."

Kate linked her arm with Sean's and smiled up at him. "Pretend we like each other," she said through her teeth.

"Don't we?" Sean countered, feigning an injured look.

Shouting questions about Brad, the covey of reporters closed around them as soon as they stepped off the porch. Kate held on to Sean and looked straight ahead, pretending not to see or hear the men and women vying for her attention. She wasn't her father's press secretary anymore; there was no reason for her to try to appease the media.

"What the hell's going on here?" Sean demanded good-naturedly, once they were safely inside his car and pulling away from the curb.

Kate pressed the tips of her index fingers to the skin under her eyes in the hope that she could keep herself from crying again. "I've just been fired from my father's staff."

"Given the sack, were you?" Sean didn't look at all sympathetic. "Best thing for you, love," he said cheerfully. "Now maybe you can be somebody besides your father's daughter."

Kate bristled. "What is that supposed to mean?"

"You've given the senator all your time and half your soul, Katie-did. When were you planning to live your life?"

Sean's words cut close to the bone, and Kate hugged herself in an unconscious gesture of self-defense. She wondered how he could have discerned something like that when they'd spent so little time together.

In that moment, Kate felt like a life-size paper doll. She had no real interests, beyond the senator's career, no hobbies and very few friends. She folded her arms, utterly demoralized.

"There now," Sean said soothingly. "It'll all come right in the end."

Kate turned her attention to him. It was better than thinking about herself. "What were you doing at my parents' house?" she asked.

Sean seemed to have a definite destination in mind, and it wasn't Kate's building. "Actually, I was looking for you. Good old Brad's arrest was all over the news this morning, and I thought you might need a sympathetic shoulder. When you didn't answer your telephone, I guessed that you were probably with your dear old dad."

Kate was beginning to rally a little. "Where are we going?" she wanted to know. The car was speeding along the freeway now; they were leaving downtown Seattle far behind.

"Simmons Field," Sean answered. "I told you I wanted to take the plane up again."

"You're not expecting me to go, are you?"

Sean grinned fetchingly. "Sure. We can have lunch at thirty-seven thousand feet—that is, if you don't mind airline food."

"Me? I'll stay on the ground, thank you. I'm no test pilot."

"That's okay, love. We only need one of those, and I'm it."

Kate sighed. "I'm not dressed for this," she said, grasping at straws. She wasn't afraid to fly, but she didn't like the idea of going up in anything that had to be tested.

"It's a passenger jet, Katie-did—not a barnstormer. Come on, live a little."

Kate nodded grudgingly, and Sean's grin widened. He looked pretty pleased with himself.

They arrived at Simmons Field, and Sean parked the sports car in a space marked Reserved. His eyes moved appreciatively over Kate's trim figure when she got out of the vehicle and stood facing him.

"I could wait for you in the hangar," she offered.

Sean shook his head and drew her close. It felt natural and right to walk within the curve of his arm. "Don't be a coward, Katie-did. I'll take care of you."

Every woman's secret dream, Kate thought sadly, recalling how she'd thought Brad would take care of her. The truth was, there weren't any princes out here, though some of the frogs could do a pretty good imitation of one. "I can take care of myself," she said firmly.

Sean made no comment on that. Soon they were mounting the portable stairway that would take them into the gleaming jumbo jet he wanted to test. There was a flight attendant on board, along with a copilot and a navigator.

Kate followed the three men into the cockpit, where she buckled herself into a seat near the door. Sean winked at her before sitting down at the controls. She bent far to one side to watch as he put on a set of earphones and then reached up to flip a variety of switches. The craft roared to life, and Kate wondered if there was an ignition key, like in a car.

She gripped the armrests on either side of her as the plane began taxiing down the runway. She could hear Sean talking to the tower in a rhythmic, practiced voice, and she relaxed a little. Even her father would have conceded that Sean was an excellent pilot.

There she went again, measuring her opinions against her father's. She forced herself to relax, realized her eyes were squeezed shut and opened them to see Sean grinning at her around the side of his seat.

Kate made a gesture with the back of her hand, encouraging him to turn his attention back to the friendly skies, and he laughed as he complied.

The navigator smiled at her from his position close by. "Relax," the older man told her. "He probably won't stall it out with you aboard."

"Stall it out?" Kate squeaked. She didn't like the sound of that. "What does that mean?"

"Never mind," said the navigator.

Kate gripped the armrests again.

An hour later, Sean landed the airplane at Simmons Field, and Kate let out her breath.

A group of bald, smiling men wearing off-the-rack suits met them on the tarmac. "Well, Mr. Harris, what do you think of our baby there?" one of them asked, gesturing toward the sleek silver aircraft.

Sean's expression was strictly noncommittal. "The engines grab a little when you stall it out," he remarked.

Kate swallowed. She'd figured out what that phrase meant, and she wondered if she'd had a near-death experience and never even noticed.

One of the officials recognized Kate. "Aren't you Senator Blake's daughter?" he asked.

Kate winced. Maybe Sean was right; maybe she didn't have any other identity besides that one. She nodded, not knowing what else to say.

"I don't mind telling you," the man beamed, looking at Sean again, "that the senator has been a very good friend to Simmons Aircraft."

Sean's expression was bland. "No worries, mate," he said. "We might be able to deal in spite of that."

Kate bit back a grin.

Sean took her hand, said a polite goodbye to the contingent from the sales department and started off toward his car.

"There's a good day's work," he said happily, opening the door for Kate. "Now we can play." He glanced at his watch. "How about some lunch?"

Kate realized with some surprise that she was hungry. Due to the stresses of a political campaign and an engagement, she hadn't had an appetite in months. She nodded.

They went to a nearby steak house, and while Kate gravitated to the salad bar, Sean ordered something from the menu.

When his plate arrived, Kate stared at it in horror. It was a T-bone steak, and it was definitely rare. "Do you know what red meat does to your heart?" she asked.

Sean rolled his eyes. "Don't tell me you've turned into one of those curmudgeons who eats sprouts and drinks blue milk."

Kate speared a cherry tomato and popped it into her mouth. "It doesn't hurt to be health conscious," she said.

Sean cut into his slab of bloody meat, lifted a piece to his mouth and chewed appreciatively. His eyes slipped briefly to Kate's breasts and then rose to her lips, where they lingered for several unsettling moments. "No worries, love," he said. "I promise you, I'm healthy."

Even though Sean had not said anything out of line, Kate felt her cheeks color. Where this man was concerned, she was nineteen again, full of crazy needs and self-doubts. She dropped her gaze to her salad, but Sean's chuckle made her look back up at his face.

"What?" she demanded, nettled.

"I've missed you, Katie-did," he said.

Kate didn't know what that meant and was afraid to ask. She hadn't suspected that Sean ever thought about her, let alone missed her. "I guess you knew I had a major crush on you," she commented.

He reached out, placed an index finger under her chin and lifted it. "I was flattered," he told her.

She felt her cheeks heat up again. "You were my sister's husband," she reminded him, feeling the old guilt rise up within her.

"It's no sin to care about somebody," he reasoned, and for just a moment, shadows flickered in his eyes, sad and dark. Kate knew he was thinking about Abby, and she felt like an intruder.

"Did you love my sister?" she asked.

"Once," Sean answered, and there was no more talk of past loves after that. They finished their meal, and Sean drove Kate back to her building. He was parking the car, while she waited near the elevator, when Brad appeared.

He looked terrible. There were dark smudges under his eyes, his hair was mussed and he needed to shave. "How could you do it?" he rasped. "How could you sell me out like that?"

Kate automatically retreated when he took a step toward her. He lunged in a burst of rage, and Kate screamed when his hands closed painfully over her shoulders.

The next thing she knew, Brad was sailing backward, colliding with one of the concrete pillars that supported the floors above.

Sean had finished parking the car.

3

Brad raised himself cautiously from the floor, one hand on his jaw. He was glaring at Sean, but he spoke to Kate. "It didn't take you long to replace me, did it?"

Kate was shaken. A brutal headache was taking shape behind her eyes. Beside her, Sean was silent, though she could feel his fury. "Please," she muttered, avoiding Brad's eyes. "Just go away."

She saw her former fiancé sway slightly on his feet and caught the scent of liquor. It was early afternoon and Brad was drunk.

"Thanks to you," he said, "I might be going away for a long time. Didn't I mean anything at all to you, Kate?"

Unconsciously, she moved a little closer to Sean, but she met Brad's gaze without flinching. "I didn't turn you in, Brad," she said. The elevator arrived then, and she stepped into it.

Sean followed, while Brad stared at her from outside.

"I won't forget this, Kate," he vowed.

Kate covered her eyes with one hand and sank against the back wall of the elevator the moment the doors were closed. "Damn," she whispered. Her stomach began to churn as the headache intensified.

Without speaking, Sean put an arm around her. She leaned against him, too shaken to resist.

When they left the elevator at her floor, Sean held out his hand. "Let me have the key," he said softly.

Dazed, Kate found her key ring in the bottom of her purse and handed it to him. "It's the one with the number engraved at the top," she told him.

Sean opened the door, then surprised Kate by lifting her into his arms. "It's time somebody made a bit of a fuss over you, love," he said huskily, carrying her inside.

Kate didn't even think of resisting when he carried her to the bed and laid her carefully down on top of the comforter. He spoke soothingly as he took off her shoes and tossed them aside, then massaged her calves.

She wondered how Abby could ever have described this man as cruel.

He left her, and she heard the door of the medicine cabinet open and close in the bathroom. Soon he was back with a glass of water and a couple of aspirin.

Kate swallowed the pills gratefully and fell back to her pillows with a little moan. She rarely took aspirin because it always knocked her out.

When she awakened, the room was full of shadows, and Sean was stretched out, fully clothed except for his shoes, on the bed beside her. His hands were cupped behind his head, and he appeared to be asleep.

Kate gasped at the rush of sensations that washed over her, and lay down again. She was afraid to move or speak, in case Sean would awaken and leave her.

After a long time she became aware that he was already awake, despite the fact that his eyes were closed.

"Feeling better, Katie-did?" he asked in a low voice.

Kate licked her lips. She could feel the hard heat of his body to the marrow of her bones, and she was terrified of what she might betray when she spoke. "Much," she managed.

He opened his eyes and turned onto his side. Lightly he brushed her lips with his own, and rested his hand just beneath the fullness of her breast. "Good," he said.

Kate barely held back a whimper as he brushed his thumb over her nipple. "Sean," she whispered, and the word was a plea. She wanted him to touch her, and *not* to touch her.

He kissed her thoroughly, as he had the night before in his car, his lips mastering hers, his tongue foreshadowing an invasion of another kind. Kate eased her arms around his neck and responded with everything that was in her.

She did not want to think of how wrong she'd been before when she'd fallen in love with Brad Wilshire.

Presently Sean pushed aside her jacket and began opening the tiny pearl buttons on her blouse. She tensed, arching her back in a spasmodic surrender, when he pushed up her bra and cupped a naked breast in the warmth of his hand.

"Please," she whispered. Please stop, please go on, please be the man I believe you to be.

Sean slid downward and took her pulsing nipple into his mouth in a bold suckling kiss. Kate cried out, entangling her fingers in his hair to press him closer.

He reached beneath her skirt, grasping her through the thin material of her panty hose, forcing her to spread her thighs for him. He spoke quietly as he caressed her and, fevered, she put her hands behind his head and drew him back to her breast.

He chuckled as he nipped at the quivering peak.

Kate, always cool and professional, was out of control. Between the stimulation of her breast and the masterful motions of his hand, she was losing her mind. She thrust her hips upward, and Sean immediately peeled her panty hose down to the middle of her thighs. She longed to part her legs, but she couldn't, and Sean took immediate advantage of her position.

Then, with the same finger, he invaded her. She sobbed his name and dug her heels into the bed so that she could lift herself to him. All the while suckling and plying her with his thumb, Sean worked her into a frenzy.

"Take me," she pleaded, clutching him. "Oh, Sean, please—please—take me!"

He left her breast to nibble and kiss the length of her neck. "Not this time, Katie-did," he said, just as Kate exploded and became a part of the sunset.

Her body jerked with sweet aftershocks for several moments, then she fell, exhausted, to the comforter. Sean withdrew his finger, caressed the pulsing bit of flesh where a lifetime of pleasure lay waiting to be shared, then raised himself on one elbow to look down at her. After studying her face, as if to memorize it, he kissed her and then sat up.

Sensing that he meant to leave her, Kate scrambled into a sitting position and laid her hands on his shoulders. "Sean, make love to me."

He shook his head once and then drew gently away from Kate to stand with his back to her. "Giving you pleasure is one thing," he said in a hoarse voice. "Taking it is another."

Kate was completely confused. She hadn't had a whole lot of experience with men, but she knew Sean wanted her as much as she wanted him. Her fingers were awkward as she tossed away her panty hose and tried to button her blouse. "I—I wanted to give myself to you."

At last he turned to face her. "I know you did, sweet," he said, "but you're not ready for that."

Kate gave up on her blouse and went to the closet, keeping her shoulders straight. "I'll be thirty years old in two weeks, Sean," she said, finding her pink terry cloth bathrobe. Turning, she tossed it onto the bed and began undressing. "Just how ready do I have to be?"

Sean looked at her the way a starving man looks at meat as she deliberately stripped away her jacket, her blouse, her tangled bra and skirt. She saw him swallow convulsively when she lowered her half-slip to stand before him naked.

"My God," he whispered. "Put your robe on."

Kate didn't move.

He shoved the splayed fingers of one hand through his hair. "Katie, if you don't do as I say, I'll walk out of here right now."

She reached for her robe and put it on. The motion of her hands was quick and angry.

Sean rose out of his chair. "In two days," he said gently, reasonably, "I'll be going back to Australia. I can't make love to you and then leave you behind."

There was a sob in Kate's voice as she shrugged and asked, "Why not? Don't guys do that every day?"

"Katie, don't," he pleaded hoarsely.

It had been another awful day, and sure as hell, Kate thought, her horoscope probably promised roses and moonbeams. "You don't have to feel guilty," she said as tears slipped down her cheeks. "After all, I came on to you—"

"Stop it!" Sean rasped, rounding the bed and grasping her by the shoulders. She winced, since Brad's hold had bruised her earlier, and saw her own pain reflected in Sean's eyes.

He pulled her close and held her. "Katie," he said, and that one word explained everything and nothing.

A few moments later Sean released her. "I'll go and get us something to eat," he said.

Kate didn't want food, she wanted Sean, but she knew he wouldn't violate his principles by making love to her. He probably still loved Abby very much, and that would make his guilt unbearable.

When she heard the door close, Kate went into the living room, opened the curtains to let in the sparkling night view of the city and put on some soft music. Her body was still reverberating with the savage pleasure Sean had introduced her to such a short time before.

About half an hour had passed when Sean returned with take-out hamburgers, sodas and french fries. By that time, Kate had lit the gas fireplace, brushed her hair and misted herself with her favorite perfume.

Sean looked at her and shook his head. "I was hoping you would have changed into a sweat suit by now," he said.

Kate smiled. "You're lucky I'm not naked," she told him.

He shook his head again. "I don't think lucky is the right word," he observed, and the paper bags rustled as he took out the fragrant food.

"This stuff is terrible for us," Kate said, just before she took a big bite of her hamburger. She was sitting near the hearth, and Sean joined her.

He glanced at the flickering fire, then the spectacle beyond the windows, then the stereo. "Are you trying to seduce me?" he asked forthrightly.

"Yes," Kate answered, chewing.

He laughed and brushed a crumb from her chin. "I ought to turn you over my knee," he said.

"Kinky," Kate replied, wriggling her eyebrows.

Sean reached out suddenly, yanked Kate across his lap, and gave her derriere a sound but painless swat. Laughing, she struggled to sit up, and in the process her robe opened and her breasts were bared. The firelight played over them with shadowy fingers, and Sean choked on a french fry.

Kate didn't move. She couldn't have, even if she'd wanted to. It was as though the whole world, all of time and creation, was holding its breath.

Like a man bewildered, Sean reached out to touch her. She closed her eyes and let her head fall back as his fingers gently shaped her nipple. Within an instant, he drew back, and Kate trembled with humiliation, unable to meet his eyes when she felt him close her robe.

There were tears glistening along her lashes when she forced herself to look at him. "I'm sorry, Sean," she said brokenly.

He laid his hand to her cheek. "Don't be," he told her. Then he got to his feet and went to stand at the window, looking out. It had begun to rain, and the city lights were shifting, shimmering splotches of color against the glass.

Kate sniffled and rose from the floor. Carefully, almost primly, she retied the belt of her robe, as though to prevent what had already happened. She had to say something; she couldn't bear the accusing silence. "I'm really glad you were with me today when we ran into Brad.''

Sean didn't look at her. "Does he have a key to this place, Katie-did?'' he asked.

Kate supposed she deserved the kind of disrespect that question indicated, but she still had some pride. She lifted her chin. "What if he does?'' she countered.

"If he does, I'm staying the night,'' Sean answered, glaring at her over one shoulder. "He might decide to come back here and avenge his honor or some such rot.''

Recalling the way Brad had grabbed her, Kate shuddered. She'd seen a side of the man in the past twenty-four hours that she'd never suspected was there. "He might,'' she agreed.

Sean was examining the couch. "Does this thing fold out?'' he wanted to know.

"Why?'' Kate retorted. "Are you tired?''

He pointed a finger at her. "Yes,'' he answered. "And you stay away from me, sheila.''

Kate wanted to scream and throw things. After all, *she* hadn't been the one to start all this.

She stormed across the room, picked up the newspaper that had been delivered earlier and turned to the horoscope page. She could expect everything to go her way that day, according to the prediction.

"Sure!" she yelled, wadding up the paper and flinging it down.

Sean's mind was not on the business of buying a fleet of airliners. He'd already read all the reports and blueprints and, most important of all, he'd taken the plane up several times. He was relieved when the last meeting with the Simmons Aircraft people ended and he was free to leave.

He was behind the wheel of his rented sports car, loosening his tie with one hand and turning the radio dial with the other, when the news story broke. Senator John Blake had suffered a heart attack en route to Washington. He was in critical condition in a Seattle hospital.

Even in the days when things were still good between him and Abby, Sean and the senator had not been friends. Abby's lies and the kidnapping attempt against Gil had made things infinitely worse. For all of that, Sean was sorry to hear the news.

His first concern was Kate. She was a little fragile these days, given the falling-out with her father and the broken engagement. She was probably pacing in some waiting room, feeling guilty as hell.

He pulled out into traffic and headed in the general direction of the hospital mentioned on the newscast. When he arrived, there were news vans everywhere, along with a small contingent of reporters. He pushed his way through and strode up to the admissions desk.

"I'm Senator Blake's son-in-law," he told the clerk.

The young woman gave him a look of mingled appreciation and skepticism. "I'll just check that out, if you don't mind. Your name, sir?"

"Sean Harris," he answered, watching the woman press a sequence of numbers with a long manicured finger. That told him all he needed to know, but he waited politely while she relayed his name to someone on the other end of the line.

"That was Ms. Blake," the receptionist said. "She says it's all right for you to come up. It's suite 4102. We have to be very careful, you understand..."

Sean nodded impatiently and walked to the elevators.

Kate was waiting for him when he got off. She was dressed in jeans and a yellow cotton shirt, and her dark hair fell free around her shoulders.

Her beautiful blue eyes were swollen from crying, and she kept running her palms down the legs of her jeans.

Wordlessly Sean held out his arms, and she flew into them.

"How is he?" Sean asked after a few moments, still holding her tightly.

She looked up at him and sniffled. "The doctors think he'll be okay," she said. "If only I hadn't—"

Sean laid a finger to her lips. "Don't say it, Kate. Don't even think it. The senator's heart attack wasn't your fault."

She drew back from him, but caught his hand in hers. "I wish I could be so sure of that," she said.

Sean wanted to take her home with him, to shelter and spoil her, to make love to her endlessly. She'd done what a long line of models, businesswomen and stewardesses hadn't been able to manage—she'd won his heart. A fraction of a moment before she'd swung her purse at that mugger's head, before Sean had realized who she was, he'd fallen in love.

He took Kate by the arm and ushered her to a plastic sofa, where they both sat down. Mrs. Blake was probably in the room with her husband, and no one else was around except for a couple of members of the senator's staff.

Kate was studying Sean's face. "You have to go back to Australia," she remembered with a note of resignation in her voice.

He nodded. Gil would be expecting him back, and the other members of Austra-Air's board of directors were anxious to hear his report on the new jet. He'd spent two nights on Kate's couch already, and he couldn't protect her forever, even though he wanted that more than anything.

"Did you have the locks changed?" he asked, worried about Brad Wilshire and his temper.

Despite everything, a grin formed on Kate's pale, fine-boned face. "I didn't need to," she confessed in a mischievous whisper. "Brad never had a key. I just wanted you to stay."

The knowledge made Sean happy, though he tried to hide it. It wasn't proper to jump up in the air and shout for joy when somebody was suffering from a heart attack just a few walls away. "Let's have a promise that you'll come and see us," he said softly, curving one finger under her chin.

She ran her tongue over her lips. "That'll depend on how Daddy is," she answered.

"He's made of iron, love," Sean assured her. "He'll be mean as ever in a few days."

Kate lowered her eyes, and Sean hoped devoutly that she wasn't retreating back into that one-dimensional identity she'd cultivated. "Maybe," she said.

Sean kissed her lightly on the forehead, and then they sat in companionable silence, holding hands and waiting.

An hour later a doctor came out and told them the senator was conscious and asking for his daughter. There was every reason to believe he'd recover.

With a small cry of relief, Kate flung her arms around Sean and squeezed. The embrace ended too soon, for she was anxious to see her father.

Sean glanced at his watch. If he hurried, he could still catch his plane. He would have to stop at Kate's to pick up the rest of his things, but that wouldn't take long since he'd never really unpacked.

"Goodbye, love," he said gently, touching her cheek.

"Your things—you'll need a key—" She rushed to find her purse and gave him her spare set.

A feeling of immense loneliness swept over Sean as he walked to the elevators. He made a point of not looking back; he knew she wouldn't be there.

Two weeks after the senator's heart attack, he was at home, preparing to return to Washington, where one of his aides had been voting as his proxy. Although things were better between Kate and her father, she still had no intention of going back to work on his staff. She didn't know exactly what she was going to do with the rest of her life but, for once, she planned to be the one who made the decisions.

Her passport, complete with a six-month Australian visa, was in the mailbox when she arrived home from visiting her parents one afternoon. She was really going to do it. She was going to pack her bags, buy an airline ticket, get some traveler's checks and fly to Australia to see Gil.

As for what had happened—or *almost* happened—between her and Sean, well, that had been nothing more than a momentary lapse. A reaction to her disappointment over the breaking of her engagement. Whenever she thought about that night, she was grateful that Sean had been too much of a gentleman to take advantage of her pain and confusion.

"Bring the boy back with you," her father instructed her the next morning when she stopped by the house on her way to the airport.

Kate sighed. "I can't just grab him and throw him on an airplane," she pointed out. "I promise to take lots of pictures, though, and if Sean will let me, maybe I can bring Gil here for a visit."

"Just get him here. There's an election coming up in November, and I want to be seen as a family man."

Kate bent to kiss her father's wan forehead. "Don't get your hopes up," she warned. "Sean doesn't trust you, and he's not likely to do you any favors."

"He has a lot of gall, keeping a man from his own grandson. This wouldn't be happening if my Abby were still alive, that's for sure. She wouldn't stand for it."

The senator's words seemed to imply some lack in Kate. "Abby is dead," she reminded him gently.

She saw the old pain move in his keenly intelligent eyes. "Yes. And as far as I'm concerned, we have Sean Harris to blame for it."

Kate knew there would be no point in arguing in Sean's defense. To the senator, it would be like trying to vindicate the devil. "I'll see you when I get back. Don't overdo."

The senator was already reaching for the telephone. Kate gave him a fond half smile and left the room.

Her mother was waiting in the hallway.

"I know I told you you should get away," she began immediately, "but I really wasn't thinking of any place so far off!"

Kate squeezed her mother's perfectly manicured, lotion-scented hand. "I'll be fine, Mother."

"That's what Abby said," Irene fretted, "and look what happened to her."

Kate sighed. She had known her older sister better than anyone except, perhaps, for Sean. While Abby had certainly looked like an angel, she'd been spoiled and selfish, too, and her temper had been quick. Kate kissed her mother's cheek. "Goodbye, Mother," she said.

Irene caught at her arm when she started toward the door. "When will you be back?"

"I don't know," Kate answered honestly.

Hastily Irene embraced her daughter. She was not an effusive woman, and the gesture was decidedly awkward. "There'll be another man along soon, dear," she promised, completely misreading Kate's emotions as usual. "You mustn't let breaking up with Brad get you down."

Kate let the comment pass. "I'll see you soon, Mother," she said, and then she was outside and the warm June sun was on her face.

It was winter in Australia, but she didn't care. She would be far away from old entanglements there; she would be able to think clearly and decide what to do with the rest of her life.

The night breeze was cool and fragrant as Kate stood on the balcony outside her hotel room, watching the dark ocean reach out to the pale sand and then slowly fall away. She would spend just this one night in Honolulu before traveling on to Fiji, Auckland, New Zealand, and, finally, Sydney.

She thought about Gil. Judging by the picture Sean had given her parents, the boy was a handsome blonde with his mother's wide brown eyes. She hoped he was more like Sean than Abby.

Below, the hotel pool sparkled like a huge aquamarine, and island music wafted up from the open doors of the lounge. On impulse, Kate decided to go for a swim. Quickly she changed out of her white cotton nightgown and into her sleek new one-piece swimsuit. Then, wearing a blue eyelet cover-up and carrying a towel, she took an elevator downstairs.

The sound of friendly laughter came from inside the lounge as Kate approached the shimmering pool. She looked up at the tropical moon, and for a single moment, her loneliness almost overwhelmed her. She plunged into the water to escape it, and when she surfaced, she felt more hopeful. After a short swim, she climbed out of the pool, dried off and ordered a mai tai to carry back to her room.

Four tractor salesmen from Iowa were in the elevator with Kate, and they invited her to their party. She declined politely and got off two floors below her own.

When she finally arrived in her room, the message light on her telephone was blinking. For a moment she was afraid. Suppose her father had had another heart attack? Suppose this time he'd died?

Kate forced herself to call the main desk. "This is Kate Blake in room 403," she said evenly. "Do you have a message for me?"

The operator asked her to wait for a moment, and Kate heard paper shuffling.

"Yes, Ms. Blake," came the answer. "You had a call from Mr. Wilshire in room 708. He'd like you to contact him immediately."

Kate felt cold all over, as though she'd just plunged into the pool again. She managed a strangled thank-you and slammed down the receiver.

Brad was here, in this very hotel. Obviously he'd followed her, and he'd jumped bail to do it.

Kate peeled off her suit, showered and put on a sundress and sandals. When she'd combed her hair, she hurled the few things she'd unpacked back into her suitcase, called the desk and asked that her bill be prepared. She would spend the night at the airport.

When Kate opened the door to leave, however, Brad was standing in the hallway, smiling at her. "Maybe we can still have a honeymoon," he said.

4

Kate resisted an urge to flee back into her room and slam the door. Brad would be delighted to see that he'd intimidated her. "I thought you weren't supposed to leave the state," she said evenly.

Brad was dressed for the tropics in white slacks and a lightweight sport shirt to match. He folded his arms and smiled ingratiatingly. "The charges against me have been dropped because of insufficient evidence. The person who turned me in wasn't—" he paused, searching his mind for the right word "—reliable."

Kate's opinion of the judicial system plummeted. She indicated her suitcase and said, "Well, congratulations to you and apologies to society in general. I was just leaving. Sorry there's no time to talk."

Brad's gaze swept over her. "I'm not going to give you another chance after this, Kate," he warned. "Either you marry me right away, or we're through."

"Don't look now," Kate answered, "but our relationship has been over since the night of the opera. So, if you'll excuse me—"

Brad shook his head, as though amazed that any woman could turn down a prize like him, and turned to walk away. Kate stepped back inside her room and bolted the door.

She slept fitfully that night, half expecting Brad to break into her room. Early in the morning she showered, dressed in slacks and a blouse and set out for the airport. After breakfast in one of the coffee shops there, she boarded Flight 187, bound for Fiji, New Zealand and Australia.

The trip was incredibly long, with layovers at each stop, and Kate lost a full day of her life when they crossed the international dateline. By the time she arrived in Sydney, she was rumpled, cranky and exhausted.

She took a cab to the hotel where her travel agent had made reservations and, after checking in and taking a shower, she collapsed into bed. When she awakened, it was nighttime, and the bridge stretching across Sydney Harbor glowed in the rainy darkness. Seeing the dense traffic still filling the lanes, she guessed it was still evening.

She was wildly hungry. She called room service, then, sitting cross-legged on the bed, she dialed Sean's number.

A housekeeper answered. "Harris residence."

For a fraction of a moment, Kate didn't know what to say. Should she introduce herself as Abby's sister, Gil's aunt or Sean's friend? "This is Kate Blake," she finally said. "Is Mr. Harris there, please?"

"I'm sorry, miss," the housekeeper replied, "but he's out with friends tonight."

Kate felt a pang of jealousy, imagining Sean on a date with some other woman, but she quickly suppressed that unworthy emotion. She wanted to see Gil; his father's social life had nothing to do with anything. "Will you tell him I called, please?" she asked.

The housekeeper promised that she would and rang off.

Kate's dinner arrived, and she sat on the edge of her bed to eat, feeling strange and far from home. She'd forgotten the keen sense of isolation Australia could give a person—especially when that person was traveling alone.

After wheeling the service cart out into the hall, Kate read for a while and then went back to sleep. A knock at her door awakened her early the next morning.

Never at her best at that hour, Kate scrambled awkwardly out of bed, stumbled over to the door and tried to focus one eye on the peephole. She couldn't see anyone, and was just about to turn around and stagger back to bed when another knock sounded and a young voice called, "Auntie Kate? Are you in there?"

Kate's heart hammered against her rib cage. She wrenched the door open and there stood seven-year-old Gil, looking up at her with Abby's eyes. He had his mother's hair, too, and Sean's infectious grin.

Until that moment Kate hadn't realized how badly she wanted to see and hold this child. With a cry of joy, she enfolded the little boy in a hug, which he bore stoically, and then ruffled his golden hair. "Am I ever glad to see you," she said. "Where's your dad?"

Gil pointed one finger toward the elevators. "He's gone to get a newspaper," he said.

Kate appreciated Sean's attempt to give her a few minutes alone with his son. She just wished they'd called first, so she would have had time to dress.

Gil sat on the bed while she dashed into the bathroom to put on jeans and a turquoise pull-over shirt. She was barefoot, both hands engaged in working her hair into a French braid, when she came out.

"You don't look anything like the pictures of Mom," Gil observed, watching Kate with quizzical eyes.

Of course, he would have been too little to remember Abby. A momentary sadness overtook Kate. "Your Grandfather Blake used to call her his Christmas-tree angel," she said.

"What did he call you?" Gil asked with genuine interest, and Kate realized for the first time that her father had never given her an affectionate nickname. He called her Kate if he was pleased with her and Katherine if he wasn't.

"Just Kate," she said.

"Dad calls you Katie-did," Gil announced. This time Kate noticed that several teeth were missing from the endearing grin.

She searched her mind for something to say to a little boy. "Do you like to play baseball?"

Gil squinted, then shook his head. "Soccer," he said. "And cricket."

There was a light rap at the door, and Kate went to open it. When she saw Sean standing there, tall and handsome in his jeans, polo shirt and windbreaker, her heart skipped and her breath swelled in her throat.

"Hi," she finally managed to say.

His green eyes danced. "Hello, love," he responded. "May I come in?"

Kate remembered herself and stepped back. "Sure," she said, feeling like an adolescent.

"We woke her up," Gil commented, from his seat on the edge of Kate's crumbled bed.

Sean's gaze was as soft as a caress. "Sorry."

Kate bit her lower lip. "It's all right," she replied lamely.

Sean smiled at her nervousness. "Get your bags packed, Katie-did, and we'll take you out of here. Plenty of room at our place."

Kate hesitated. Seeing Sean again, she knew she hadn't really dealt with her feelings for him at all. It would be so easy to be wanton. "I . . . I wouldn't want to impose," she said quickly. "I mean, I can just as well stay here."

Gil looked so crestfallen that Kate went to sit beside him on the bed. She draped an arm around his shoulders. "What's this? A sad face when I've just come all the way from America to see you?"

"Let's take your Aunt Kate out for some breakfast," Sean suggested quickly. He looked as disappointed as Gil.

Since it was drizzling, Kate took her raincoat. They left the hotel and walked through the clean, modern streets to a small coffee shop that Sean seemed to know.

A hearty breakfast made Kate feel better—and more adventurous. "Maybe I could stay with you for a little while," she said to Gil, "if you're sure I won't be intruding."

Gil's coffee-brown eyes were alight. "I'll show you my dog, Snidely," he exclaimed, beaming. "He can roll over and play dead."

"I'm very impressed," Kate told him. "What else can he do?"

Gil's expression turned sheepish. "Not much else, besides chew shoes and make messes in the garden."

Kate laughed. "He sounds like a regular dog to me."

"Except for Georgie Renfrew, he's my best mate," Gil said.

Sean winked at Kate from behind the rim of his coffee cup, and she was absurdly pleased, as though he'd made some grand gesture.

They left the coffee shop several minutes later, and Kate held Gil's hand as they walked back to her hotel. There, she packed her things and then checked out. She, Sean and Gil took a cab to Sean's house in an elegant section of Sydney.

It was as wonderful as Kate remembered, with a view of the harbor and the Opera House, and her room was a small suite, with its own bath and a real wood-burning fireplace. The carpets were a pale blue, the bedspread was a complementary floral print, and there was even a small balcony outside.

"It's beautiful," Kate told Sean softly, but she was already regretting her decision to stay in this house. The place had belonged to Abby first, just as the man had, and Kate felt like an intruder.

Sean touched the tip of her nose. "I see ghosts in your eyes. What's the problem, Katie-did?"

Kate bit her lower lip and turned away. In the distance she could hear a dog barking with unbounded glee. Evidently Snidely and Gil had been reunited. "I'm just a little tired, I guess," she lied.

Gently Sean turned her to face him. "And feeling just a little guilty, I think."

Kate nodded, not trusting herself to speak.

Before Sean could say anything more, Gil bounded in with a huge, hairy dog of some indeterminate breed.

"This is Snidely," he said, glowing with pride.

Snidely offered a yelp in greeting and then rolled over on his side to lie completely still. Kate supposed he was playing dead.

"Good dog," she said to please Gil.

"Take him outside before Mrs. Manchester sees him," Sean ordered.

Reluctantly Gil led the animal out of Kate's room.

Sean traced the outline of Kate's cheek with one index finger. "We'll talk later, love, when you're settled in and rested."

Kate nodded.

Sean bent his head and kissed her lightly on the lips, and Kate was almost knocked off her feet by the jolt that passed between them. In that moment she would have given her soul to lie beneath Sean, to share her body with him.

But he left her standing in the middle of that beautifully decorated room, listening to the patter of winter rain against the windows.

Kate was curled up in a chair, reading a paperback she'd brought with her on the plane, when the housekeeper rapped at the half-open door and stepped inside the room. Mrs. Manchester was a heavily built woman with friendly blue eyes and salt-and-pepper hair pulled back into a loose chignon. She smiled at Kate and went to the hearth to build a fire.

"Nothing like a cheery blaze on a wet day," she commented, dusting her hands together and looking back at Kate as the fire crackled to life. "Would you like some tea, miss?"

Kate shook her head. "No, thank you," she said, and an unexpected yawn escaped with the words.

"Seems to me you might want to lie down and take a nap," Mrs. Manchester observed. "Traveling so far takes such a lot out of a person."

The bed did look comfortable, and the dancing flames on the hearth gave Kate a cozy, protected feeling. "I think you're right," she said, and kicking off her shoes, she crossed the room to stretch out on the bed.

Mrs. Manchester kindly covered her with a beautiful knitted afghan and slipped out, closing the door behind her.

Kate drifted off to sleep and dreamed of a campfire under a sky ablaze with silver stars. There, in that imaginary world, Sean lay beside her, his hand on her breast. She whimpered and stretched, wanting more of his touch.

"Kate." His voice penetrated her dream, low and husky.

She stretched again, still asleep, still needing.

She felt his fingers at the buttons of her shirt. Cool air whispered over her skin as he took away her bra. The feel of his mouth on her hardened nipple brought her awake with a start.

Although Sean was in the room, he was standing by the fireplace, and Kate was still fully dressed. Her disappointment was keen.

"That must have been a pretty erotic dream," he said, throwing another log on the fire before approaching the bed.

Kate blushed in the relative darkness of the room, but her words were bold. "It was. You were making love to me beside a campfire."

"Rest assured, Katie-did," he said, bending to kiss her forehead, "I'm not about to make love to you."

Kate glared up at him. "Why not?" she asked, insulted.

"Because the guilt would eat you alive," Sean answered. "For you at least, there would be three of us in the room—you, me and Abby."

Kate closed her eyes. As much as she wanted to cry out that he was wrong, she knew he wasn't. She tossed back the afghan and sat up.

"Mrs. Manchester made tea," Sean said, indicating a wheeled cart sitting beside the fireplace.

Apparently they were going to pretend they hadn't discussed sex. Kate smoothed her hair and disappeared into the bathroom for a few minutes. When she came out, she had recovered her dignity.

She sat down in one of the two wing chairs facing the hearth and poured tea from a small china pot into a matching cup. There were strawberry scones, too, and various cookies she knew Sean would refer to as biscuits. Kate took a raspberry scone, even though she normally didn't eat sugary foods.

Sean was leaning against the fireplace mantle, watching Kate as though she were a complex puzzle. "Why are you here?" he asked.

Kate took a sip of strong tea before answering, "I wanted to see Gil, of course."

"If that were all of it, you'd have been here a long time before now."

Avoiding his gaze, Kate reached for a cookie. The man made her nervous, and when she was nervous, she ate. She shrugged. "I guess you could say I'm looking for myself," she replied. Her indigo eyes rose of their own accord to his face. "You were the one who said I needed a life of my own."

Sean poured tea into the second cup, added generous doses of sugar and milk and sat down in the chair across from Kate's. "Are you serious about that?"

Kate nodded. "I turned thirty a few days back, Sean, and look at me. I've never been married, never borne a child, never even worked at a real job that I landed on my own."

"And now you're out for an adventure?"

Kate considered for a moment. "Something like that."

Sean set his teacup down in its saucer. Even in the firelight Kate could see the mischief dancing in his eyes. "I think I can provide you with one of those," he said.

Before Kate could think of a response, Gil burst into the room with Snidely loping at his heels. "Mrs. Manchester's gone out to see her sister," he explained, "so I brought Snidely inside straight away." He glanced at the scones and biscuits.

"Have one," Kate said, watching him with delight.

Gil hesitated, looking to his father for permission. Sean must have given it silently, for the boy closed one grubby hand around a scone. After saying thank you and breaking off a small piece for Snidely, he ate hungrily.

"Are you going back to America soon?" the child asked when he'd disposed of the scone.

"I don't think so," Kate said, wondering if Gil was anxious for her to leave. She was probably disrupting some planned excursion with her unexpected visit.

"I hope you stay a long time," Gil responded. "You're not scared of Snidely and you don't go 'round saying he smells. I like that in a woman."

"It's certainly a trait I always look for," Sean agreed, deadpan.

Kate laughed and rumpled Gil's hair. "Well, I happen to like a discerning gentleman," she said.

"We'll try to dig one up for you," Sean replied.

Snidely was following his own tail in an endless circle. Outside, the winter rain drizzled against the windows, and the fire crackled on the hearth. Kate wanted to stay in that room with Gil and Sean forever.

As it happened, though, Sean rose out of his chair and said, "We'll leave you to yourself for a while. Dinner's in a couple of hours."

Kate wondered if she was supposed to dress up. It didn't seem likely that dinner would be formal when Mrs. Manchester was out of the house.

Feeling rumpled from her nap, she took a long, hot shower. Then, not knowing what was expected of her, she got into a striped caftan in shades of pink and a pair of sandals. She wore her dark hair down and applied a small amount of makeup.

Sean's eyes lit up when she walked into the living room. He was wearing slacks and a beautiful cable-knit sweater, and his dark hair caught the light of the fire.

"Now I'm sorry we're having dinner at home," he teased, deliberately intensifying his accent. "I could make all me mates jealous if I showed you off."

Kate laughed, but his words pleased her. It had been a long time since she'd felt so attractive.

Sean offered white wine, and she nodded. When he brought her the glass, she asked, "Where's Gil?"

"He'll be along when he's done with his bath. Like as not, Snidely's in the tub with him."

Kate laughed again at the picture that came to her mind, and then took a long sip of her wine because she felt so nervous inside. It was as though she'd regressed from thirty years of age to thirteen, and she couldn't for the life of her think of anything intelligent to say. She followed the sip with a gulp.

Sean was just about to say something when Gil bounded into the room, looking scrubbed and handsome in short pants and a white shirt. "May I stay home tomorrow and look after Kate?" he asked with a hopeful lilt in his voice.

"Actually, no," Sean responded immediately.

Gil's disappointment was only momentary. After an instant, he was smiling broadly again. "Well," he said, "if you're going to be that way about it—"

"I am," Sean assured him.

Watching her nephew, Kate was thinking how much her parents would enjoy knowing him. She made a mental note to approach Sean, when the right moment arrived, about letting the boy visit.

The three had a simple dinner of meat pies and salad left behind by the very efficient Mrs. Manchester, and then Gil went off to do his homework. The next day was Monday, and school would be back in session.

"I'm sorry I haven't asked you before, Kate—how's your father?" Sean asked as they sat at a small table in a glass alcove, watching the rain fall.

"He's getting better every day," she answered. She studied Sean, wondering if she dared mention the possibility of a visit from Gil in the same sentence with her father. She decided against it. "I called home as soon as I arrived at the hotel, and Mother said he was almost ready to go back to Washington."

Sean turned his wineglass in one hand. "Have you let them know you're here?" he asked.

"I called the hotel and left word at the desk," she answered, yawning. "If any messages come in, they'll call me."

"You're still not over the jet lag," Sean remarked. "You'd better get some sleep."

"Will I see you tomorrow?"

Sean shook his head. "Not until late. I've got business meetings all day."

And Gil would be in school. A feeling of loneliness swept over Kate, and she lowered her eyes.

Unexpectedly Sean put his hand under her chin and raised her face. "Come away with me, Kate," he said hoarsely, getting to his feet and drawing her to him. "I'll show you the adventure of a lifetime."

Despite all her fine resolutions, Kate was powerless in his arms. Something melted deep inside her at the memory of that afternoon's erotic dream. "What kind of adventure?" she asked, her eyes wide as she looked up at him.

"I've got a little plane. I could show you some of the outback."

The idea intrigued Kate more than she would have dared to admit. "What about Gil?" she asked. "Would he go along, too?"

Sean shook his head. "He's got a school trip coming up. We could go then."

"When?" Kate wanted to know. She felt herself melting like a candle as Sean gently caressed her breasts.

"Day after tomorrow," he answered on a long, weary breath.

Kate closed her eyes. She wanted Sean to bare her as he had that other time on her bed at home, but she knew he wouldn't. He was only torturing her, and himself. "Just the two of us," she mused aloud. "Interesting."

Sean bent his head and nibbled the covered peak of one breast. It went taut between his lips. "It'll be very interesting," he promised.

Kate was burning inside. The guilt she'd felt earlier was fading. Sean had a right to happiness, and so did she. No law, moral or civil, said the two of them had to stay apart for fear of defaming Abby's memory. "I think I should go back to my hotel," she said.

Sean lifted his head quickly, his green eyes full of questions. He voiced only one. "Why?"

"Because there I wouldn't feel as though Abby's watching me from beyond the veil," she answered.

"Gil won't understand," Sean reasoned.

Kate didn't want to do anything to hurt her nephew, especially when she was just getting to know him. "You're right," she conceded, deflated.

"There's another place we could go," Sean said thoughtfully. "Wait here."

Kate sat watching the fire and willing her agitated body to calm itself. Presently Sean returned, his hair sparkling with droplets of rainwater, accompanied by a teenage girl.

"This is Angie," he said to Kate. "She lives across the way, and she's Gil's favorite baby-sitter. Angie, this is my good friend, Kate Blake."

The pretty blond girl smiled at Kate. "That I am," she said. "Gil's favorite baby-sitter, I mean. Pleased to meet you, Miss Blake."

Kate nodded to the girl, but she was looking at Sean.

He beckoned to her with one hand, and against her better judgment, she stood and took his hand.

They were inside his car, a British sports model with a canvas top, and speeding down the drive-way before Kate could catch her breath. She certainly hoped Sean didn't fly the way he drove.

"Where are we going?" she finally asked when it was clear that no explanation was forthcoming.

"You'll see," Sean answered.

A few minutes later they pulled into the parking garage of a towering building overlooking Sydney Harbor and the Opera House. Kate looked at Sean questioningly as he hauled her out of the car and strode off toward a bank of elevators, still gripping her hand.

"Sean!" she protested.

Inside, he pulled her close and kissed her so thoroughly that when he drew back, she was momentarily disoriented. He chuckled and kissed her again.

"Where are you taking me?" she demanded when she could gather the breath to speak.

The elevators whisked open on a small, beautifully decorated lobby. "This is the penthouse," Sean explained at last. "My company keeps it for visiting dignitaries."

Kate lifted an eyebrow as he unlocked the door. "Is that what I am?" she teased.

Sean winked. "Austra-Air wants to make sure your stay in Oz is memorable," he assured her. Then he opened the door, and Kate stepped into the penthouse, instantly bedazzled.

The outside walls were all glass, and Kate could see, through the rain, the lights of the bridge and the Opera House and the ferry boats crossing the water. All around them, in fact, lay the city like a kingdom made of colorful jewels.

"Oh, Sean, it's magnificent," Kate whispered.

He closed and locked the door. "So are you," he whispered, drawing her close again.

She reveled in the muscular hardness of his body as he bent and nibbled softly at her neck. When she was nearly too weak to stand, he led her into the darkened living room, where huge couches and hassocks sat in the shadows. He removed her caftan with a minimum of trouble, pleased to find she was wearing only panties beneath it.

Kate groaned as he laid her out on one of the large hassocks, the city spread before her like a gift, and eased her panties down over her hips. Something nagged at her—the realization that she'd been so wrong about another man in what seemed to be another lifetime—but she couldn't break free of Sean's spell. It was entirely too powerful.

"Do you want me to love you, Kate?" he asked.

"Yes," Kate managed to whisper. "Oh, yes."

Gently he lifted her legs so that they rested over his shoulders. His hands caressed her inner thighs. "Prepare for some slight turbulence," he teased.

5

After a few minutes of Sean's loving, Kate was frantic for fulfillment. A delirium of pleasure caused her to writhe and toss her head from side to side even as she pleaded, "Sean—I don't want to—not without you . . ."

Breathing very hard, he stripped off his sweater and tossed it away, then got to his feet. He lifted Kate into his arms and carried her into a nearby bedroom.

Her skin, covered with a fine film of perspiration from her exertions, felt deliciously cool. She watched her man as he removed the rest of his clothes and then came to her.

"Kate," he whispered hoarsely, just before his lips covered hers in a masterful kiss.

She responded with her whole being, her doubts falling away behind her like the tail of a comet. The throbbing heat in her body was building toward a crescendo again, and she began to twist and thrash beneath Sean. She was wildly impatient.

He buried his face in her neck, chuckling. "So it's like that, is it?" he teased in a husky rasp.

Kate arched her back, and in that moment, Sean's control snapped. He found and entered her in one fiery stroke.

For Kate, for that instant, all of creation froze like the slides in a broken kaleidoscope. In the next, the universe splintered into colorful pieces, for she had been too greatly aroused and too long denied. Her body bonded itself to Sean's, and with a primitive cry, she gave of herself, body and soul, in the age-old way of women.

Her triumph excited Sean, and with a groan, he began increasing his pace. Kate urged him on with soft, breathless words and the motions of her hands. She met each thrust with a swift rise of her hips, taking him far inside her.

He muttered something that might have been either a prayer or a curse when the quest became urgent, and then, with a hoarse shout, he stiffened, gasping her name.

Her hands soothed the moist, muscle-corded expanse of his back. "I'm here," she whispered.

Sean trembled violently as he surrendered what nature had decreed he must, then sank down beside Kate on the bed of shadows. "God," he muttered. "My God."

They lay still and silent for a long time, and then Kate started to rise from the bed. Sean immediately pressed her back down.

"I'm not through with you yet, love," he told her. "Not nearly."

Kate gave an involuntary groan as he found her breast in the darkness and weighed it in the palm of his hand. His thumb moved over the responsive nipple, shaping it. Preparing it.

She twisted onto her stomach, gasping, knowing she needed a few minutes to rest. But Sean was granting no quarter; he reached beneath her, and she flung back her head like a wild mare when he found what he sought.

"Stop," Kate murmured, even as she ground her hips in an involuntary response.

"Not until you're satisfied," Sean replied.

Kate could not turn onto her back again, for she was trapped by her own needs. "Oh, Sean— Sean—"

"Almost there," he told her, intensifying his efforts to drive her mad. "Almost there..."

Kate was damp with perspiration from her head to her feet. Her legs were stiff and wide apart, and her toes curled into the bedspread, seeking purchase. Her hands were pressed against the mattress, raising her upper body from the bed. "Oh," she cried, lifting her eyes to a ceiling she couldn't see. "Oh—*oh* . . ."

"It's going to be a long night, love," she heard Sean say gently from somewhere beyond the exploding lights and shooting flares of her climax. "A long, sweet night."

Kate awakened feeling as though she were lying in the light of a gentle sun, her sated body wrapped in the softest silk. Expertly Sean had put her through her paces, draining away all her tensions.

He bent and kissed her. "We'd better go, love. Mrs. Manchester will get the idea we're up to something."

Kate laughed and then stretched. "I don't think I can move from this bed," she said.

"That's fine, too," Sean answered. He was fully dressed again, but he pretended he was about to take off his sweater.

Kate bounded out of bed and hurried into the bathroom. One more session of Sean's singular brand of loving would turn her into a madwoman for sure.

She took a hasty shower and got back into her panties and caftan, which Sean had thoughtfully brought from the living room. He was there when she came to him, looking out at the city lights and sipping from a crystal glass.

"What's that?" Kate asked.

"Vodka," he answered.

Kate wrinkled her nose. "Bad for you," she said.

"We're fresh out of carrot juice," Sean explained. "Let's go, love."

They took the elevator down to the parking garage and walked to Sean's car. When Kate was seated in the passenger seat, Sean walked around to the driver's side and got in. The engine roared to life and Kate felt sad to be leaving a place that had been hers and Sean's for a house that had been Abby's.

"I'll sell the house," Sean said, and Kate was convinced he'd been reading her mind. "It's that simple."

"It isn't, and you know it," Kate argued. "You have a child—my sister's child. I live in one hemisphere, and you live in another. There are just too many differences."

"What about tonight?" Sean argued. "Was that a difference?"

Kate swallowed. "A few more nights like tonight and I'll be a candidate for a nursing home.

I must have had six . . .'' Her cheeks went hot as she fell silent.

"Seven," Sean replied, "but who's counting?"

"That was only physical," she said. "You can't build a relationship on that." She prayed Sean would say he loved her, so she could tell him her real feelings for him.

"Come on, Kate. Men and women have been building 'relationships'—I hate that word—on *that* for a few million years." He shifted gears as they began moving uphill. "Beware of me, Katie-did—now I know how to bring you right into line."

Kate's face throbbed with renewed heat, and she was grateful for the darkness. "That was a chauvinistic thing to say!"

"Nevertheless," Sean replied with a shrug, "it's true."

And it was, although Kate would have died before admitting it. All Sean had to do was maneuver her into certain positions, touch her in certain ways, and she was lost.

"The way it is with us," he began after a long silence. "Was it like that with Brad?"

Kate knew he was really asking if what they had was new to her, so she didn't resent the question. "Brad and I never made love," she admitted, "so I wouldn't know."

Sean pulled the car over to the side of the street and stopped so suddenly that Kate was stunned. "What?" he demanded.

"I said, Brad and I never made love—"

"How the hell did you manage that? You were engaged to the man!"

Kate's eyes were very wide. "You sound angry."

A closer look proved that he was more indignant than angry. "I feel so cheap," he said.

Kate couldn't help laughing. "I think that's supposed to be my line," she told him.

"You were saving yourself for marriage with him," Sean pointed out. "With me, it's a fast roll in the straw and 'thank you very much I've got a plane to catch'!"

Kate only shook her head, baffled.

Sean wrenched the car back into gear and pulled onto the road again, muttering a swear word.

Kate squinted at him in the darkness. "Did I miss something here? I haven't been to bed with anyone since college, and you're upset because you're the first?"

"Who was he?" Sean barked.

"Who?" Kate countered, getting angry herself now.

"The guy in college!"

Kate laughed again. "My God, I don't believe this!"

Sean's hands tightened on the steering wheel, then relaxed again. "Were you in love with him?"

Kate sighed, turning her eyes to the rain-misted view. Even in that weather, at that hour of the night, it was magnificent. "I thought so. His name was Ryan Fletcher, and we were going to be married."

"What stopped you?"

"Abby brought you home, and I realized what love really was."

Sean was quiet for a moment, then he said something that surprised Kate to the core of her being. "I married the wrong sister, I think."

Kate reached out and laid a hand on his thigh. She felt the muscles tighten to a granite hardness beneath her palm. "What went wrong between you and Abby?" she asked. "You were so happy once."

"Maybe I was. Abby changed her mind about life with me about five minutes after our plane took off from Seattle. She didn't like being married to a pilot, she didn't like sex, she didn't like Australia.''

"Why didn't she leave you, then, and come home?"

Sean gave Kate a sidelong look. "This was home," he said flatly.

"Not to Abby," Kate pointed out.

"And not to you," Sean replied.

"We're not talking about me," Kate countered.

"I think we are," Sean argued. "You couldn't stay here with me and be happy any more than Abby could. You're a Yank, and you belong in the States."

Kate sighed. "I'll decide where I belong, thank you very much."

"You belong in my bed," Sean answered, "and if you think you can deny me, I'll have to prove my point."

Kate knew better. Sean could take her anytime, anyplace he wanted; her responses were evidence of that. All the same, her pride made her keep a defiant silence.

They had reached Sean's house, and the garage door opened at a command from a button on the dashboard. The inside was only dimly lit.

Kate started to get out of the car, but Sean stopped her by gripping her wrist in his hand. He gave her a soft, savage kiss. When it was over, her knees were so weak that she could hardly walk inside the house on her own, but she wouldn't let Sean support her. He'd done quite enough.

In her room, Kate quickly undressed and put on a flannel nightshirt. She brushed her teeth and climbed into bed, determined to sleep.

She couldn't. For much of the night she relived the things she and Sean had done together, and by morning she needed him again.

With Sean in meetings and Gil in school, Kate had a day strictly to herself. The first thing she did was place a call to the United States, using her credit card.

Her mother answered on the second ring. "Hello?"

"Hi, Mother," Kate said, feeling shy with this woman, as though they were strangers with little common ground. In many ways, of course, they were exactly that.

"Kate," Irene confirmed, sounding a little annoyed. "Well, how is our world traveler?"

Kate suppressed a sigh. "I'm fine," she replied. "How are you and Daddy?"

"I'm very well, thank you, and your father is almost his old self again. We're off to the house in Washington tomorrow, as a matter of fact. Have you seen Gil?"

"I'm staying in the same house with him. He's a wonderful boy, Mother."

"Of course he is," Irene answered, sounding impatient. "He's Abby's child, isn't he?"

Kate could not have explained the emotions her mother's words aroused in her, and she was glad she didn't have to. She was also glad to be more than ten thousand miles away. "I think Sean had something to do with the project," she pointed out.

Irene sighed. "Which brings me to the most obvious question of all. What are you doing staying under that man's roof?" She made it sound as though Kate had taken a room in hell in order to have regular chess matches with the devil.

Kate thought of the sweet torments Sean had subjected her to the night before and wanted him more than ever. It was all she could do not to answer, *I'm here because I'm addicted to his lovemaking.* "It's a big house, Mother," she said instead. "They've got lots of room. Besides, this way I can be close to Gil."

"I'm not at all sure your father will approve. You haven't taken up with that man, have you?"

"*That man* has a name. It's Sean."

"Very well then, Katherine—are you involved with *Sean*?"

Kate wanted very much to answer yes, but she didn't quite dare to do it. "I'm his friend," she said, and her lips curved into a wry smile as she thought what an understatement that was.

"He's a monster—directly responsible for your sister's death."

Kate closed her eyes. "You know that isn't true, Mother. You remember what the coroner said. She'd been drinking and taking pills."

"Only because Sean Harris drove her to it. Australian men are chauvinists, Katherine. They use you up and throw you away when they're finished."

"I didn't call to argue about Australian men," Kate said firmly.

"Don't hang up!" Irene said quickly.

"We may not be the best of friends, Mother," Kate answered, "but we haven't reached that point."

"Your father will want to know whether or not you'll be bringing Gil back to the States and when."

Kate was developing a headache. "I haven't spoken to Sean about that yet. I need time."

"Just remember that your father isn't getting any younger, and he has a weak heart. It would mean the world to him to see his grandson."

Guilt swept over Kate like an ocean wave, but she stood strong against it. It wasn't her mission in life to effect a reunion between her parents and Gil. "I'll do my best," she said. "Goodbye, Mother."

"Goodbye, Katherine," her mother responded.

It would have been easy for Kate to lapse into a low-grade depression at that point, but she was determined not to let Irene get her down. She hung up and went to find Mrs. Manchester.

After conferring with the housekeeper about the best places to shop, Kate called a cab and ventured into downtown Sydney. Most of the stores were in Pitt and George Streets, and she was soon happily embroiled in purchasing the things she would need for her mysterious adventure with Sean. She bought several pairs of jeans, heavy flannel shirts, special underwear, socks and hiking boots. Then, lugging her bags, she found a model airplane for Gil, a fancy collar for

Snidely, a book for Sean and a small box of imported chocolates for Mrs. Manchester.

It was midafternoon when she arrived back at Sean's house, where Gil and Snidely met her at the gate.

"I was afraid you'd gone back to America without saying goodbye," Gil told her.

Kate shifted all her packages so that she could ruffle his hair. "I'd never do that," she said gently. "Didn't Mrs. Manchester tell you I was out shopping?"

Gil shook his head. "All she said was to keep Snidely out of her clean house," he said. His brown eyes took in the bags she carried, one of which was clearly marked with the name of a local toy store. "What have you got there?"

"Help me get them inside and I'll show you," Kate answered, handing over half her burden to her nephew.

He accepted graciously, and the two of them went as far as the screened porch, Snidely at their heels. They dropped the bags and boxes on a wicker sofa, and Kate handed the model airplane to Gil.

His brown eyes widened. "Thank you, Aunt Kate," he said, accepting the gift.

"I believe the American word is 'wow,'" commented a quiet masculine voice from the inner doorway.

Kate looked up and saw Sean, and she went warm all over.

"Wow!" crowed Gil.

Kate felt almost shy, despite the fact that she'd thrashed beneath this man's hands and lips and body the night before. "I bought something for you, too," she said, handing him the book. It was an illustrated history of aviation.

"Thanks, Kate," he said. He accepted the book.

"And I didn't forget Snidely or Mrs. Manchester, either," Kate announced, perhaps too brightly. She felt awkward and inept all of a sudden.

Sean set aside the book to help a delighted Gil put the new collar on the dog. Moments later the boy rushed off to the kitchen to present Mrs. Manchester with her chocolates.

"What else did you buy?" Sean asked. The way his green eyes touched Kate made her feel a special intimacy with him, a deep need for more of what they had shared in the night.

Kate shrugged. "Jeans and shirts to wear when we go away," she said.

Sean was very close now. "Smart girl," he said. His hands rested on the sides of Kate's waist; his lips were a fraction of an inch from hers. "Did you buy a sexy nightgown?"

Kate eyes widened. "No," she admitted.

He gave her a light, nibbling kiss that set her senses afire. "Good, little sheila, because you aren't going to need one."

Kate trembled at the portent of his words. She was afraid and excited, wanting to run away and to stay, both at the same time. "Are you making an indecent proposal?"

Sean kissed her again, more thoroughly this time. "Absolutely," he answered, supporting Kate when her knees went limp beneath her.

She looked up at him, dazed. If he'd led her off to bed at that moment, she would have gone willingly, even eagerly, but he didn't. He gave her a swat on the bottom and nodded toward the bag of clothes she'd bought for their trip. "You'd better wash those before you wear them," he said, "or the sizing will make you itch like crazy."

Kate batted her eyelashes at him. "Thanks. I never would have thought of that on my own."

He gave her another swat and helped her gather up the bags. They were in the laundry room, cutting off tags and poking things into the washer, when Mrs. Manchester arrived, shooed them off and took over the project herself.

Sean took Kate's hand and led her into the living room. Since it was a bright, sunny day outside, there was no fire burning on the hearth, but Kate knew there would be later. Winter nights in New South Wales were cold.

"Where are we going on this adventure of ours?" Kate asked, perching on the arm of a comfortable sofa upholstered in practical navy blue corduroy while Sean poured himself a drink.

"Queensland," he answered. "To a place out beyond Lightning Ridge."

"But it's winter," Kate reasoned.

Sean winked at her. "No worries, love. I'll keep you plenty warm of a night, and sometimes in the daytime, too."

Kate blushed and lowered her eyes. She could hardly wait to leave. "We'll go tomorrow?"

Sean nodded. "Can you wait that long, little sheila?"

Kate glared at him. Sometimes he carried his caveman routine just a little too far. "I can wait forever."

"Don't make me prove you a liar," Sean said, grinning. Then he set aside his drink and approached her.

Kate's breath caught in her throat when he placed gentle hands on both sides of her face and kissed her, his tongue claiming her almost as masterfully as his manhood had the night before.

"Maybe I'd better take you to bed," he said softly when the kiss was over and Kate was still trying to regain her balance.

Kate trembled. His delicious threat was empty, since Gil and Mrs. Manchester were home. Wasn't it?

Sean chuckled at her bemusement and gave her another soul-rendering kiss. When it was over, Kate had to sink down onto the couch, since she couldn't stand on her own any longer.

Gil came bounding in at that moment like a fresh breeze, carrying the box that contained his new model airplane beneath one arm. "Can we put this together tonight, Dad?" he asked eagerly, his brown eyes shining as he looked up at his father.

Kate felt such love for both Sean and Gil in that moment that she couldn't have spoken past the lump in her throat. Tears of emotion glistened in her eyes, but if Sean noticed, he pretended otherwise.

"We could get a start on it, I suppose," Sean agreed. "Have you got all your things packed for the trip to Canberra?"

Gil nodded. "Mrs. Manchester took care of that," he said.

With a wink at Kate, Sean took the colorful box his son was holding out to him. "This looks like a three-man job to me," He said. "Want to help?"

Kate wanted to be near both of them. "Sure," she said with a sniffle.

Gil squinted at her. "Are you crying, Aunt Kate?" he asked.

Kate shook her head. "Yes," she said, contradicting her own gesture.

"Women," commented Gil.

Sean laughed, and even though he didn't touch Kate in any way, she felt as though she'd been held and comforted.

The three spent a happy evening putting the model airplane together, although Sean complained that it was a job Wilbur and Orville Wright wouldn't have wanted to tackle. By the time dinner was served, the plane was only half-finished.

"Looks like the rest of this will have to wait until you get back from your trip, mate," Sean told his son. "You've got lessons to do, haven't you?"

Gil nodded and went off to wash his hands before supper. When he joined Sean and Kate at the table, he was already yawning. "I'll bring you back a present from Canberra," he promised Kate. His eyes flickered to his father. "And you, too, Dad," he added.

"Thanks for remembering," Sean said with a grin.

Gil sighed contentedly. "This has been the best night since my birthday," he said.

Again Kate felt silly, sentimental tears stinging her eyes. She quickly lowered her gaze to the delectable seafood salad on her plate. In that moment she mourned all the birthdays and Christmases she'd missed with Gil, just as though he were her own son.

Sean's hand closed over hers, though only momentarily. "You're tired," he said.

Kate nodded. That was true enough. She'd never really recovered from jet lag, and then she'd spent most of the previous night in Sean's arms.

Sean's voice was almost unbearably gentle. "Maybe you'd like Mrs. Manchester to bring your dinner to your room? After all, it'll be an early morning tomorrow."

Kate wouldn't be pampered. She ate what she could of her dinner before excusing herself to hurry off to her room. After a brief shower, she collapsed into bed without even putting on a nightgown.

6

That night was cold, but the next day dawned bright and warm. As Kate sipped the bracing tea Mrs. Manchester had brought to her, she looked ahead to the trip she and Sean planned to share and wondered what had possessed her to agree to it. She was not the daring type, as a general rule.

Abby had been the bold one. She'd been the one to skydive, get a pilot's license and go off to Australia to live with a new husband. Kate wondered what had changed her sister from a fearless woman to a little girl writing petulant letters home but refusing to do anything about her situation.

A knock on her bedroom door interrupted Kate's musings, and she uttered a distracted, "Come in."

It was Mrs. Manchester, back for the tea service. She smiled at Kate and waited politely for an indication that she was through.

"You didn't work here when my sister was alive, did you?" Kate asked the older woman, frowning. "I'm sure I'd remember you."

Mrs. Manchester hesitated. Her warm eyes skirted Kate's. "I was here when she died, miss," she finally answered. "I'd just taken over from Mrs. Pennwyler."

"Is she still around anywhere, this Mrs. Pennwyler?" Kate asked. "I'd like to talk with her about Abby."

Mrs. Manchester shook her head. "Sorry, love. The old girl, bless her soul, has gone to live with her eldest son up in Darwin. He's got just one eye, you know. Hurt in the war."

"What do you remember about Abby?"

"Mrs. Harris was very unhappy, miss."

Kate nodded. "I know. She wrote often. But I've never understood why she didn't divorce Sean—Mr. Harris—and catch a plane home."

"She had problems," the housekeeper said sadly.

Kate nodded, thinking of the coroner's report. A chill swept over her as she imagined what it must have been like for Abby hurtling off a high cliff that way, knowing she was going to die within seconds.

Mrs. Manchester was putting Kate's cup and saucer and the plate that had held a flaky croissant onto a tray. "Mustn't let the dead get in the way of the living," she said wisely. "Our time is limited enough as it is."

For the first time since she'd started thinking about Abby, Kate smiled. "You're right," she agreed. "Is Mr. Harris up yet?"

Mrs. Manchester laughed. "Up? He's been out and about for hours, miss—just got back a few minutes ago."

Kate looked down at her jeans, flannel shirt and hiking boots as Mrs. Manchester left the room. She hoped she was dressed for whatever Sean had planned.

As if summoned by the mere thought of his name, he appeared, looking around the door at Kate. There was an appreciative glint in his green eyes. "Everything's ready, love," he said.

A tremor of mingled delight and fear went through Kate as the man she loved stepped into the room. Like her, he was wearing jeans and a casual shirt. He carried a slouchy leather hat in one hand. "How do I look?" she asked.

"Good enough to eat," Sean responded hoarsely, and another shiver went through Kate even as her skin flushed hot.

She cleared her throat and averted her eyes for a moment, feeling shy again. "What about Gil? Did he leave on his field trip?"

"While you were still sleeping, sheila," Sean said. One moment he was in the doorway, the next he was standing so close to Kate that she could feel the heat of his body. He traced the outline of her mouth with a light touch of his index finger.

Kate trembled visibly, and her response embarrassed and angered her. "I could still back out, you know," she pointed out.

Boldly Sean cupped his hand over one of her breasts. The nipple hardened beneath the stroking of his thumb. "Could you?" he countered.

Kate groaned. "That isn't fair," she managed to say.

Sean was unbuttoning her shirt. Beneath it she wore a stretchy undershirt, rather than a bra, and her breasts and nipples were clearly visible through the thin fabric. Sean admired them for a long moment while Kate's cheeks flared pink. Although she was outraged, she was unable to stop him.

With one finger, he drew the neckline of the undershirt down until one breast was exposed, plump and vulnerable. "Just a little taste of

what's going to happen when I get you alone,"
Sean said, and when he bent and touched Kate's
nipple with the tip of his tongue, she tensed with
sudden, violent pleasure. All thought of rebel-
lion gone, she cupped her hands behind his head
and pressed him to her.

But he was only playing. He abandoned the
bare breast and turned to the one covered by the
undershirt. Through the fabric, he nipped at it,
grazing it lightly with his teeth, and Kate cried
out softly, her head falling back.

Again she was disappointed. Sean caressed her
naked breast once before covering it again, then
he rebuttoned her shirt. She had never been more
frustrated in her life.

"Sean, I need you," she managed to say.

He gave her a kiss as exciting as his dalliance
with her breasts had been. "Later, little sheila."

Kate ached. "Now," she said.

Sean chuckled and gave her trim backside a
swat. "Later," he repeated.

Kate was furious. Sean had aroused her on
purpose and now he was just going to leave her
to suffer. "I want you now," she insisted.

"Tough," Sean replied. He grasped Kate by
the hand, taking up her suitcase with the other.
She allowed him to lead her through the house

and out into the driveway where an open Jeep was parked.

"Damn you," she whispered angrily. "I want you to drop this Tarzan routine right now!"

Sean tossed her expensive suitcase into the back of the Jeep as though it were bargain-brand stuff. Then, grinning down at Kate, he lifted her by the waist and set her down inside the vehicle.

Although her pride dictated that she get out of the Jeep, storm into the house and call a taxi to take her back to the hotel, she buckled the seat belt instead.

Sean put the hat on and got behind the wheel. Looking over one shoulder, Kate noticed he'd brought a lot of other things besides her suitcase. She saw a tent, a single sleeping bag, fishing poles and a lot of packaged food, among other things.

"How come there's only one sleeping bag?" she demanded.

Sean grinned at her as he shifted into reverse. He was looking back at the road when he answered, "Spoiling for a fight, aren't you, sheila? Well, watch out, because you're about to get one."

Kate glowered at him and folded her arms across her chest. Her breasts still tingled from

Sean's earlier attentions. He was a skunk, she decided, to get her excited and then leave her high and dry. "I wouldn't lower myself," she said.

"We'll see about that," Sean quipped, and then they were moving rapidly down the left hand side of the road.

Kate gasped, forgetting for a moment that all Australians drove that way. Sean put a hand on her thigh. Although Kate knew the gesture was meant to relax her, it only heightened her tensions.

"It'll be all right, Katie-did," he shouted over the noise of the wind.

Kate pushed his hand away and folded her arms again. That made Sean laugh.

They didn't attempt to speak after that. Instead, they raced through traffic rapidly, leaving the sprawling city behind. After an hour they reached a small airport.

Kate felt as though the breath had been buffeted from her. Her hair, so carefully plaited into a tidy French braid, was flying wildly about her face. Before looking at Sean, she grimaced into the side mirror to make sure there were no bugs in her teeth.

Sean caught her by surprise when he lifted her from the Jeep. Her body brushed the length of his as he lowered her to her feet, and the ache within her intensified until it was nearly unbearable.

"I ought to slap you," she said.

He kissed her until her knees were weak. "Patience, little one," he told her gruffly. "We're spending tonight on a friend of mine's station. You can do all your lovely little tricks for me when we're alone."

Kate decided then that she definitely *would* slap him. She raised her hand to do so, but Sean caught her by the wrist and pulled her close. She was breathless.

Sean kissed her forehead lightly. "Behave yourself," he ordered. Then he left Kate and started unloading the things in the back of the Jeep.

For lack of a better idea, Kate helped. He stowed the tent inside a small twin-engine airplane and went back for more baggage. Once they'd loaded the plane, he got inside and started the engines, then walked around the small craft, making a mysterious examination of everything.

Thinking she might lose her courage if she didn't take definite action, Kate climbed onto the wing, the way she'd seen Sean do, opened the passenger door and got into the seat.

Sean was wearing earphones now, and tuning in the radio. "Buckle up, love," he said to Kate.

She fastened her seat belt, trying not to think about how small and fragile that airplane seemed. As far as Kate was concerned, it was almost as flimsy as Gil's model. She bit down hard on her lower lip and clasped the edges of the seat in both hands.

Sean was talking with the control tower, but Kate didn't listen to his words. Her whole life was passing before her eyes.

Soon the plane was lumbering and jolting along the rough pavement toward the single runway. Kate closed her eyes tight and prayed silently for some last-minute reprieve, like a flat tire or an empty gas tank.

God was not listening to Kate's prayer. The airplane gained the runway and began taxiing along it at an ever-increasing speed.

"Open your eyes, Kate," Sean said reasonably, although he had to speak in a loud voice to be heard over the roar of the engines.

Kate obeyed him, not because of any desire to see, but because her first impulse was always to do just as Sean said. She was going to have to work on that, or she'd end up fetching his slippers and lighting his pipe. "Oh, God," she cried.

Sean laughed as the little craft hurtled into the sky. The ground fell away beneath them while they climbed toward the clouds.

Kate's knuckles were beginning to ache. She released her grasp on the seat and let out her breath. An exhilarating sensation of freedom and excitement had overtaken her horror, and her eyes went wide as she looked down upon farmhouses and fields.

"It's beautiful!"

"I know," Sean answered. They had gained enough altitude, it seemed, for he was leveling the plane off now. He muttered something into the speaker on his earphone and then grinned at Kate. "Control says they're glad you like it," he told her.

Kate made a mental note to watch what she said from then on. There were things she wanted to say to Sean that were none of Control's business. She rolled her eyes at him and gave him a shaky smile.

They'd been flying for over an hour when Sean switched the radio off and removed the earphones.

Kate was alarmed. "Don't you need to stay in contact with the tower?" she asked.

Sean smiled indulgently. "We're too far out for that, love," he said.

"Oh," Kate replied, and she was smiling, too. There were thoughts of revenge in her mind. "I suppose there's no reason I can't repay you for all the frustration you've caused me, then, is there?"

Sean looked a little worried. "I don't know what you're talking about," he said.

Kate unfastened her seat belt and turned sideways. "You will," she promised.

Sean stiffened and gave an involuntary groan as she ran her hand lightly up his thigh.

And that was only the beginning.

By the time the trees and craggy cliffs beneath them had given way to open grassland, Sean was as disconcerted and unsatisfied as Kate. He gave her a hard look as she settled back and refastened her seat belt.

She smiled at him. "How do you like the taste of your own medicine, Mr. Harris?" she asked.

"I'd step lightly if I were you, sheila," he told her. His jaw was clamped down tight, and he shifted uncomfortably in his seat. "As you Yanks like to say, you're on thin ice."

Kate tilted her head to one side. "Just what is it you're threatening to do to me?" she asked sweetly, batting her eyelashes and clasping her hands together beneath her chin. "Beat me? Strip me naked and leave me for the dingoes?"

Sean gave her a wry look. "Wrong. Except, of course, the part where I strip you naked. I like that one."

Kate laughed. "I think we're even," she said.

"Do you? Well, two can play at your game, sheila." With that, he reached out and laid his hand on her upper thigh. She tensed as his fingers brushed her most sensitive and private place. Even knowing that he had no intention of satisfying her, any more than she'd satisfied him, she couldn't bring herself to push him away.

She felt a thin layer of perspiration cooling her heated skin. "Sean," she whispered as he tormented her with touches as light as the passing of a butterfly.

He chuckled. "The poet was right. Vengeance is sweet."

"I hate you," Kate gasped, even as her body jerked slightly in response to the whisper-light forays of his fingers.

"Absolutely," he replied.

"Oh," Kate moaned.

"Open your shirt, Kate," Sean said quietly. His tone was warm and inviting and terribly seductive. "I want to look at you."

"No," she murmured breathlessly, even as her fingers rose awkwardly to the buttons of her shirt and began working them.

When her shirt was open, Sean's fingers moved to her breasts. Their peaks strained against the fabric of her undershirt, longing to be free.

"You know what I want now, Kate," Sean said with a gentle kind of sternness that heated Kate's blood to a passionate simmer.

She did know, and it wasn't in her to refuse, even though she knew Sean was only dallying with her. He would leave her unsated until they were in bed that night, and that was hours away. With both hands, she raised the undershirt so that her breasts were bared for Sean's gratification.

He made an appreciative sound low in his throat and began to caress and shape her. With a groan, Kate sunk her teeth into her lower lip and turned her head, looking down at the distant ground, searching for anything that would distract her from Sean's delicious torment.

Half a dozen kangaroos hopped along the grassy ground, moving more rapidly than Kate had ever dreamed they could. She moaned as Sean continued to fondle her, arching her back even as she searched her mind for a way to rebel.

The plane began a gradual descent, and Kate scanned the horizon. There was no sign of a station anywhere in sight. She couldn't even see a single sheep.

"What are you doing?" she asked.

Sean withdrew his hand in order to concentrate fully on the controls. "You win, sheila," he answered cryptically. "I can't wait any longer."

"But this is the middle of nowhere!" Kate cried, coming swiftly to her senses. She pulled down her undershirt and then fastened her buttons.

"The perfect place," Sean answered.

Moments later the plane was bumping crazily along the ground. "What if we can't take off again?" she asked, wide-eyed.

"In a few minutes, love," he answered, "you're not going to need a plane to fly."

Kate's muscles went limp, then tensed again, going taut as piano wire. The plane came to a stop, and she closed her eyes in relief. Her heart was hammering, and she wasn't sure whether it was the unscheduled landing that had caused it, or the prospect of Sean's lovemaking.

He opened his door and climbed out onto the wing, then jumped nimbly to the ground. Kate was still trembling in her seat when he came around, got up onto the wing on her side and opened the door.

His eyes full of mischief and promise, he kept his gaze fixed to Kate's all the while he was unfastening her seat belt and turning her to face him. Her legs dangled outside the plane, on either side of his hips.

"Oh," Kate whimpered as he began unbuttoning her shirt.

He soon had that laid aside and her undershirt up beneath her armpits. Her breasts were warm and swollen under his gaze, their peaks pouting for his attention.

She cried out in mingled relief and despair when his mouth closed over one of her nipples. "A—aren't you even going to kiss me?" she asked.

He drew back long enough to answer, "I'm past that, thanks to your teasing, sheila. Now you'll have to pay the piper."

Sean took a long time at Kate's breasts, enjoying first one and then the other. When he finally pressed her back across her own seat and his, she was almost out of her mind with need. She felt the snap open on her jeans, trembled as they slid, her panties with them, down over her hips.

Ever so lightly, Sean kissed the tangled silk that sheltered Kate's femininity from all but him. She moaned and lifted her hips as an offering, but he only teased her with more kisses. At the same time, his hands were busy removing her boots, pulling her jeans and panties down and off.

When Kate was thrashing from side to side, frantic with need, he mounted her. She felt all the familiar doubts and fears, all the old insecurities, but they weren't enough to stop her. She held her breath as he opened his zipper and freed himself. When he entered her, she became a wild thing, clutching at him with her hands and wrapping her legs around his hips.

Although she urged him to hurry, Sean's pace was slow and rhythmic. He meant to extract the last ounce of response from Kate before satisfying himself, and that knowledge only increased her frenzy.

When she was on the edge, he stopped to enjoy her breasts again at his leisure. Kate was woman at her most primitive; she pleaded, she threatened, she wheedled and bargained.

At last, with a low moan of his own, Sean gave in. He began to move more rapidly, and the friction made Kate cry out and stiffen as satisfaction overtook her. She was torn apart in those moments, and reassembled into a new, softer and gentler woman. She had been mastered, like a wild mare broken to ride, and the feeling was glorious.

Sean's release was a violent one. He lunged deep inside Kate and hurled his head back, his teeth bared over a string of savage endearments.

Kate cupped his taut buttocks in her hands as his powerful body bucked several more times, and then he fell to her breasts, gasping for air. Within moments, he was rolling a taut nipple between his lips and then suckling hungrily even as his torso heaved with the effort to breathe.

Kate plunged her fingers into his hair. She would have been content to hold him like that all day but, when he'd had a long turn at both her breasts, he raised his head and pulled her undershirt down. While he fetched Kate's panties and jeans from the wing, she hastily buttoned her shirt.

He bent and kissed both her knees before handing her the rest of her clothes. "You're a bad girl, sheila," he scolded. "Maybe that's why I like you so much."

Kate wished he would have said he loved her, but she'd long since learned that wishes were one thing and reality was very often another. "You're a scoundrel," she said, wrenching on her panties and jeans. "Where are my boots?"

Sean recovered them from the ground and handed them to her, rounding the plane as Kate shoved her feet into them.

He boarded the plane and reached across Kate to close her door, the back of his arm brushing her full breasts. "That'll keep you satisfied until tonight I hope," he said.

"Your arrogance is not to be believed!" Kate fussed.

Sean grinned broadly and quoted back some of the outrageous things she'd said to him during her climb to the heights.

"Bastard," Kate said.

The plane engines whirred and the propellers began to spin.

"Have you ever taken off from a place with no runway before?" she asked worriedly, now having something else to think about besides the obnoxious man beside her.

"Only about fifty thousand times," Sean answered, reaching for a pair of mirrored sunglasses on the instrument panel and putting them on with a flourish.

Kate was back to gripping the edges of the seat, although she was so relaxed that it was hard to hold on. She wanted nothing so much as to crawl into some warm, safe bed right there on the ground and sleep for twenty-four hours.

The plane jolted terribly as Sean increased its speed. Finally, with a rattling mechanical grunt, it flung itself into the air. Kate let go of her seat.

"I'm getting hungry," she said.

"I don't wonder," Sean answered, "considering the energy you've burned up in the past few minutes."

Kate hit him in the shoulder, but she was grinning. She felt too damn good to be angry.

After another hour in the air, an enormous flock of sheep came into view, shepherded by a man and three dogs. In the distance, Kate could make out a sizable house and a number of rustic outbuildings.

"Is that your friend?"

Sean rocked the plane from side to side, and the man below waved a hand. "Yes," he answered. "That's Blue. He's the best mate I ever had."

Kate continued to stare at the ground as Sean banked the plane into a wide sweep around the house and buildings and began a descent toward a dirt landing strip below. She could see another plane on the ground, as well as gasoline pumps and a pickup truck with rusty fenders.

"Does he live here all by himself?" Kate asked, thinking how lonely that would be. This part of Australia was so vast and empty, except for the occasional gum tree and the ever-present brown grass.

Sean shook his head as the plane nosed downward. "He's got a wife and kids."

"Kids?" Kate echoed. "Out here? Where do they go to school?"

Sean was busy landing the airplane, so he didn't look at Kate as they landed. "They don't. Ellen teaches them herself."

Any answer Kate might have made was prevented by the jostling impact of touching down.

She breathed a silent prayer of gratitude for a safe landing and unfastened her seat belt.

Sean stopped Kate before she could open the door and jump out of the plane. "Don't be trying to put any fancy ideas in Ellen's head," he warned. "She likes her life the way it is."

While Kate was still thinking what an odd remark that was, Sean shut off the engines and got out himself. He came around to lift Kate to the ground as a slender blond woman came running from the direction of the house, her face alight.

"Sean!" she cried as she reached him and flung herself into his arms.

He gave her a hug and a sound kiss on the forehead and set her down. "Ellen," he said, "meet Kate."

Kate greeted the woman with a smile and an outstretched hand, even though she was wondering why Sean hadn't mentioned that she was Abby's sister. "Hi," she said.

Turquoise eyes sparkled in a suntanned complexion. "Hello, Kate," Ellen said, accepting Kate's hand with a strong grip. Momentarily she turned back to Sean. "Did you bring me books and chocolate bars?" she demanded.

Sean laughed and gestured toward the plane where the gear was stowed. "Enough to last you six months," he answered.

Kate heard dogs barking in the distance and the bleating of sheep. Soon, Sean's friend Blue would reach them.

She looked nervously at Sean. She wondered if Blue and Ellen had been Abby's friends, too.

Sean glanced at her, and once again she had the strange sensation that he could read her thoughts. He put one arm around her waist and pulled her close, his lips moving softly against her temple.

"Tonight," he whispered.

7

When Sean had taken a large grocery box from the back of the airplane, he and Kate and Ellen started off toward the house.

It was a sturdy, practical-looking place, built mostly of natural stone. Smoke curled from two different chimneys, reminding Kate that the day was cool. She'd forgotten in the heat of Sean's lovemaking and its glowing aftermath that it was winter in Australia.

As they neared the house, three children, two girls and a boy, appeared at one end of a long, verandalike porch. "It *is* you!" one of the little girls cried, bounding down the steps to attach herself to Sean's right leg.

Sean laughed and shifted the box in his arms so that he could ruffle the child's flaxen hair. "Hello, Sarah," he said.

Now that Sarah had broken the ice, the other two children came running, too. They were introduced to Kate as John and Margaret.

"We were doing lessons," John confided. "I'm glad you're here, Uncle Sean, because it was a dead bore."

"John!" Ellen scolded, but there was a smile in her beautiful blue-green eyes.

The bleating of the sheep and barking of the dogs had grown much louder. Sean set the box down on the step and turned toward the mingled sounds, a broad grin stretching across his face. After a moment's pause, he strode off to meet his friend.

Kate started to follow and then stopped herself. Ellen was shooing the children back to their lessons.

"Come in," she said to Kate with a sunny smile. "Blue and Sean will be a while."

Kate returned the smile and went inside with Ellen, finding herself in a kitchen that ran the length of the house. Burnished copper pans and kettles hung on the walls on either side of an enormous brick fireplace. School books, pencils and papers were strewn over a long trestle table, and a rocking chair sat in a sunny alcove.

"Tea?" Ellen asked, going over to an old-fashioned electric stove and lifting a steaming kettle.

Kate was developing a taste for tea. "Yes, please," she said.

"You can sit here with us, Miss," little Sarah put in. She looked to be about ten years old.

Kate sat down at the end of one of the benches aligned with the trestle table. "Thank you," she said. She tried to look at the work the children were doing without being too obvious.

Ellen had gone back outside to fetch the box Sean had brought while the tea brewed in a blue delft pot. When she returned, she set the box on the end of the table, opposite Kate, and pulled back the flaps.

Kate watched as she lifted out boxes of chocolate bars and stacks of books. "Bless that man," she said as John, Sarah and Margaret looked at the candy with round eyes.

"Just one between you," Ellen told the children, smiling as she handed them a chocolate bar. "Mind that you break it up evenly now."

While the kids were dividing the candy, Ellen turned her attention back to Kate. "Would you like one?" she asked.

Kate shook her head. "No, thank you," she answered. She was more interested in the books.

Ellen laughed as she handed one to Kate. It was a romance novel showing a sweet young thing being swept up into the arms of a dashing buccaneer. "They're better than candy," she said. "I can't get enough of one or the other."

Kate smiled as she looked through the other books. The covers were all quite similar, depicting almost every period in history as well as the present day. At the thought of Sean shopping for these books, her smile widened.

Ellen brought the teapot to the table, along with lovely china cups, too fragile for a station in the outback. "Do you think they're silly, those books?" she asked in a lilting voice, her expression worried.

"No," Kate said quickly. "As a matter of fact, this one with the sheikh on the cover looks pretty interesting to me."

Ellen's eyes sparkled. "Doesn't it, though?" she agreed, pouring the tea.

Before Kate could make further comment, a tall man with auburn hair and brown eyes entered the kitchen, followed closely by Sean.

"And who's this?" Blue demanded good-naturedly.

When Sean answered, there was a note in his voice that Kate had never heard before. "Katie-did, meet my best mate—Blue McAllister."

Kate nodded, feeling oddly moved. "Hello."

Blue hung up his hat and lightweight leather coat before progressing to the table. "Hello," he said, helping himself to one of Ellen's cherished chocolate bars. "I suppose you have a last name, as well?" he asked. "Or is it a well-guarded secret?"

"Blake," Sean said before Kate could answer, and this time he sounded angry.

Kate wondered why.

A look passed between Sean and Blue that wasn't entirely friendly. "You were related to Abby?" Blue asked in gentle tones.

Kate nodded. "She was my sister."

An uncomfortable silence descended, and Kate found herself wondering again why she'd given in to her passions when it was so clear that she and Sean could never have any kind of lasting relationship.

It was Ellen who smoothed things over. She laid a hand on Kate's shoulder and said, "Welcome. It isn't often I get a chance to talk with another woman, except when we can raise Sally Hobbins on the radio. I'm glad you're here."

"Thank you," Kate answered, but her eyes had strayed to Sean's face, and she knew they mirrored all the questions she wanted to ask.

He turned away, ostensibly to gaze out the window. Blue suggested having a look at the starboard engine of his airplane, since it had been sputtering, and the two men left the house without a backward glance, John tagging after them when his mother nodded her permission to leave his schoolwork.

"Don't mind the men," Ellen said in her delightful accent after sending Margaret and Sarah off to play with their dolls. "I never met one yet that had half the tact he needed."

Kate wanted to cry, but she didn't. She couldn't quite manage a smile, however. "Were you and Abby friends?"

Ellen hesitated for a long moment. "Not really," she answered reluctantly. "The only time she ever came out here with Sean, she spent the whole of the weekend trying to convince me to leave Blue. Imagine it—me without Blue."

There *had* been a special spark between the McAllisters when Blue came into the kitchen, now that Kate thought of it. "Why on earth did Abby want you to leave your husband?"

Ellen sighed. "She said I was downtrodden, and that I was going to seed out here with nobody to talk to but Blue and the kids."

The remark Sean had made when they landed came back to Kate in that moment. *Don't be trying to put any fancy ideas in Ellen's head. She likes her life the way it is.* "Abby could be pretty thoughtless sometimes," she said, taking a sip of her rapidly cooling tea.

Ellen smiled and shrugged. "She didn't know how it is with Blue and me," she said, and there was something in her tone and her manner that made Kate flash back to the explosive passion she'd felt in Sean's arms a short time before.

She nodded, a little shaken by the experience.

Ellen seemed to sense Kate's thoughts. She hid another smile behind the rim of her teacup. "You're in love with Sean?" she asked a moment later, keeping her face expressionless.

Kate swallowed. "I'm afraid so," she admitted miserably.

Ellen reached out for the pretty teapot and refilled Kate's cup and her own. "Troubles?"

Kate lowered her head for a moment. "You saw how he reacted when I told Blue Abby was my sister," she said.

Ellen looked genuinely puzzled. "Yes?"

"I'm a reminder of a very unhappy time in Sean's life," Kate told her new friend sadly.

Ellen's face brightened. "I think perhaps you're another kind of reminder altogether," she reasoned. "I can't remember when I've seen Sean look so relaxed."

Kate blushed. If Sean looked relaxed, it was no mystery to her.

Ellen chuckled. "I see I've blundered in where I don't belong," she said. Then she graciously changed the subject. "Earlier you said you'd planned to teach once. What did you take up instead?"

Kate gave Ellen McAllister a grateful look. "Political science," she said. "Daddy—my father thought it would be a better use of my time and his money. He wanted me to work on his staff."

Ellen broke off a square of chocolate from the bar she'd opened earlier and laid the morsel on her tongue. A look of ecstasy flickered briefly in her eyes, then she commented, "Do you like it—working for your father?"

Kate searched her heart. "Not really," she confessed.

"If you could do anything in the world," Ellen began, narrowing her eyes in speculation at all the possibilities, "what career would you choose?"

Kate didn't have to think. "I'd be like you, Ellen—making a home for the man I love. Raising his children."

Ellen put one hand to her mouth in feigned shock. "You mean, you'd actually like to be a—" she lowered her voice to a scandalized whisper "*housewife*?"

Kate laughed. "Yes," she answered.

Ellen squinted at her and took another square of chocolate. "I can't figure you as Abby's sister," she said.

Kate knew the remark was meant as a compliment, but she felt sorry that Abby had missed having Ellen for a friend. "According to Sean, she didn't like being a wife much."

Ellen glanced nervously toward the door, looking for the men, then lowered her voice to a confidential tone. "She took a lover the first year they were married," she said.

Kate was stunned. She'd known that Abby had been unhappy from the first, but she'd never suspected such a thing. "Did Sean know?" she asked.

"Yes," interrupted a taut masculine voice from the doorway. "Sean knew."

Kate raised her eyes to his face. He looked grim and angry.

"I'm sorry," Ellen said quickly. She got up from the table and fled the kitchen in embarrassment.

"If you want to know anything about Abby and me," Sean said coldly, "ask me and not my friends."

Kate was quietly furious. "Now just a minute, Sean Harris. Don't you think you're being a little unreasonable here?"

He shoved a hand through his dark hair, and his broad shoulders slumped slightly. "Until about five seconds ago," he said hoarsely, "I thought Abby's affair was a secret."

Kate went to Sean and put her arms around him, her chin tilted back so she could look up into his face. "She was a fool," she said softly.

He kissed her forehead. "You're prejudiced, but thanks, anyway," he said.

Kate laid both hands on his chest, their torsos fitting together comfortably. "Go and talk to Ellen," she suggested. "She thinks you're mad at her."

Sean held her a little closer. "Couldn't that wait a little while? I'd like to show you where we'll be sleeping tonight."

Kate thought of Sarah and John and Margaret. "We're not going to share a bed under this roof," she said firmly. "There are children here."

Sean moved her to arm's length, his hands gripping her shoulders. "What?"

"It wouldn't be right, Sean," Kate whispered. "We're not married."

"Then we'll get married."

"You're crazy. Where would we get a license? And a preacher?"

Sean sighed. Obviously those things would be impossible to find in the middle of nowhere. "Wouldn't being engaged make it right?" he asked.

"No," Kate said stubbornly.

Sean swore. "Then I'll just have to convince Blue that we should sleep in the barn," he replied.

Kate set the last bacon, tomato and lettuce sandwich on the platter with a flourish. Lunch was ready.

She started when she heard a sizzle behind her and turned to see Ellen cracking eggs into a frying pan. Kate could barely believe her eyes. "Eggs?" she asked.

Ellen smiled at her. "Of course they're eggs, love," she answered.

Kate cast a bewildered glance toward the pyramid of sandwiches she'd prepared, then looked at Ellen again. "You don't mean we're going to eat them?"

"Of course we are," Ellen answered, raising her eyebrows.

It came back to Kate then. She remembered the Australian habit of consuming fried eggs with almost everything, and bit back a lecture on cholesterol. She didn't want the McAllisters to remember her as a meddler. "Oh," she finally answered, sounding a bit lame.

When they all sat down at the long trestle table a few minutes later, it made for a merry group. The children were all talking at once, while Blue and Sean carried on a separate conversation.

Kate's appetite diminished a little when she watched the men lift the tops off their sandwiches and add a fried egg, and she let the platter pass her by without taking one. Keeping her eyes on her own plate, she ate what she could.

When the meal was over, Kate helped Ellen with the dishes. Blue and Sean and all the children had gone outside again.

"Are you feeling all right?" Ellen asked, looking genuinely concerned. "You didn't eat much."

Kate sighed. "I'm a little tired," she confessed. "I've never really gotten over my jet lag."

Ellen's lovely eyes were full of concern. "I'll show you where your room is, and you can lie down."

Kate shook her head. She didn't want to waste a minute of this experience on anything so ordinary as a nap. After all, she might never find herself on an Australian sheep station again. "I'd like to see more of the place," she said.

Ellen was obviously pleased. "Then you shall," she promised with a bright smile. They finished the dishes and walked outside.

"That's the shearing shed over there," Ellen said, pointing out a large building. "We have about two dozen lads come to help us when it's time to crop the sheep."

The bleating of the animals filled the air, and Kate could see them spread out all around the outbuildings like a sea of dusty clouds. "Do they make that sound all the time?" she asked.

Ellen smiled. "Mostly, yes. Of course, they're generally not this close to the house."

"Doesn't Blue have anyone to help him?" Kate asked, imagining what a task it must be to drive so many sheep from one pasture to another.

Ellen squared her slender shoulders and looked just a mite offended. "He has me," she answered.

"But you've got the children to take care of, and the house," Kate pointed out.

"I still have time to lend Blue a hand when he needs me." Ellen sounded proud and a little defensive.

Kate allowed herself to imagine living in such a place with Sean and she understood. When Ellen McAllister lay down beside her husband at night, she was probably bone weary, but she had the satisfaction of knowing that the work of her hands and heart and mind made a real difference.

Kate couldn't remember when writing speeches and booking hotel reservations for her father had ever given her such a feeling. "You're lucky," she said.

Ellen relaxed. "I know," she answered.

The two women walked for some time, while Ellen showed Kate the large patch of ground where she raised vegetables, the coops with the squawking hens that produced the McAllisters' eggs and provided the occasional chicken dinner, the building where the hired hands would stay when it came time to shear the sheep.

"Don't you ever get lonely, living way out here?" Kate ventured to ask as they entered the cool, spacious living room with sturdy, serviceable furniture and a fireplace that adjoined the one in the kitchen.

A large quilting frame was set up in the middle of the room, and a beautiful multicolored quilt was in progress. Ellen touched it with a fond hand as they passed. "I've got Blue and the kids and the people in those books Sean brings," she replied, starting up a set of wooden stairs. The banister was made of rough wood with bits of bark clinging to it in places. "Most of the time they're enough."

Kate sighed. "I guess nobody likes their life all the time," she said.

Ellen nodded as she looked back. They were on the upper floor when she asked, "What do you like best about your life, Kate?"

The question took Kate by surprise, and so did the realization that she hadn't really *had* much of a life before she came to Australia. "Sean," she answered, her eyes lowered, her cheeks warm.

"It's nothing to be ashamed of, loving a man," Ellen insisted. They had reached a doorway, and she led the way inside. "This is our room, Blue's and mine."

Kate saw a lovely hardwood bed covered with one of Ellen's colorful handmade quilts. There were several comfortable chairs, and two hooked rugs brightened the wooden floor. An old-fashioned folding screen stood in one corner of the room, and a wisp of a nightgown was draped over its top.

With a soft smile, Ellen pulled down the nightgown, folded it and tucked it into a drawer.

As much as Kate liked this woman, she was filled with envy. It wasn't hard to imagine the happiness Blue and Ellen shared within the intimacy of these four walls; it was a charge in the air, like lightning diffused in all directions.

They went through each of the children's rooms, then Ellen opened a door at the end of the hall. It was a small room with a slanting roof, and contained an iron bedstead that was painted white. The spread was another of Ellen's elaborate quilts, this one in a floral design, and the curtains matched. A ceramic pitcher and bowl set was on top of an old wooden nightstand.

Kate drew in her breath. "It's charming," she said a moment later.

Ellen smiled. "I'm glad you think so, because you'll be sleeping here."

Kate was embarrassed again. "Sean . . . ?"

Ellen's eyes sparkled with amusement and affection. "He can sleep downstairs in Blue's study. There's a chesterfield there that folds out into a bed."

Kate bit her lower lip and nodded.

Ellen laughed. "I dare say he'll have his due once you're away from here, though."

Kate had absolutely no doubt of that. She wouldn't be able to resist Sean when he set his mind on seducing her, so she didn't plan to waste her time trying. She looked toward the open window, where lace curtains danced on a rising wind.

"The sky looks angry," Ellen fretted, crossing the room to lower the window sash. "A storm's brewing, I think."

Kate felt an elemental yearning to be alone in this room with Sean, to lie with him beneath the beautiful quilt and feel his arms tight and strong around her. "There must be things you need to do," she said to distract herself. "How can I help?"

Ellen remembered with a start that her wash was hanging outside on the line, and the two women ran to reach it before the rain did.

"What about the sheep?" Kate shouted over the increasing howl of the wind as she and Ellen swiftly wrenched sheets and shirts and dish towels from the clothesline.

"They don't mind a little rain," Ellen called back.

Enormous drops began pummeling the ground, the roof and the windows only moments after Kate and Ellen were inside. They stood near the sputtering fire to fold the fresh-smelling laundry. The kids were back at the trestle table, working at their lessons.

About half an hour had gone by when Blue and Sean came in from looking after the sheep. They were both soaking wet, and Ellen rushed to peel away Blue's jacket and hat. As she was leading him toward the fire, Kate's eyes met Sean's.

She longed to fuss over him in the same way, but she wasn't certain she had the right. After all, this wasn't her house and Sean wasn't her husband.

Both mischief and appeal flickered in his eyes as he gazed back at Kate. Then, rather dramatically, he sneezed.

Kate went to him. "You're wet," she said helplessly.

"And cold," he answered.

Kate shivered, although she was dry and warm. After a moment's hesitation she took his hand and led him toward the hearth. There was something sweetly primitive in making a fuss over Sean while a storm raged at the windows, and she wished they were alone.

Sean smiled and kissed her forehead, then began stripping off his shirt. Drops of water shimmered in his hair, catching the firelight like diamonds. His chest glistened with moisture.

Using all the determination she possessed, Kate turned away. "I'll get you some tea—"

"They'll be needing more than tea," Ellen said wisely. She took a bottle of brandy down from a cupboard, along with a jar of instant coffee.

Kate stood by and watched, since there was nothing else to do, while Ellen brewed two mugs of coffee and added healthy doses of sugar, milk and brandy. Kate's hands trembled a little as she carried the nutritional disaster to Sean and held it out.

He accepted the offering with a little ceremony. His eyes, linked with Kate's, seemed to strip away her dry clothes, until she felt naked in front of him. She'd lost all awareness of the others.

Sean lifted the brew to his lips and drank, and when he swallowed, Kate felt the brandy coursing through her own system, warming her, melting her muscles and bones.

"You need to lie down," she heard Sean say. The words didn't seem to go with the movements of his lips.

A moment later he set the mug aside and lifted Kate into his arms. She could feel the wetness of his skin seep through her lightweight flannel shirt.

He carried her to the room Ellen had showed her earlier and laid her gently on the bed.

"The children," she whispered in sleepy despair.

Sean grinned as he unlaced her hiking boots and pulled them off. "It's all right, Kate-did. I'm only putting you to bed."

"I wish we could—make love," Kate said with a long yawn.

Sean chuckled. "Believe me, sheila, so do I. But you're right—we can't with the nippers about."

It felt so good to have her shoes off that Kate stretched and gave a little groan, curling her toes as she did so. Sean unsnapped her jeans and slid them down over her hips, thighs and legs. It was so different from the last time he'd removed them.

He stripped her to her undershirt and panties, then tucked her underneath the quilt and bent to kiss her forehead. "Sleep, sheila," he said softly.

Kate snuggled down between the crisp, chilly covers, giving a little sigh. "It's so—nice here..."

Sean kissed her again, this time on the lips. "All the comforts of home," he agreed. "Except for one, of course."

Kate opened her eyes, but they fell closed again. She hadn't realized she was so tired. "I'm afraid of thunder," she confessed after the sky was rent by a deafening roar.

Sean drew up a chair and sat down beside the bed, holding her hand in his. "I'll never let anything hurt you," he promised.

Kate couldn't remember a time when she'd felt so safe and wanted. Her mouth seemed to be moving without permission from her brain. "I wish we lived in a place like this," she said, punctuating her words with a yawn. "Just you and me and Gil and our babies . . ."

Sean's chuckle was a rich, sweet sound. "Oh, love, you are making it hard for me to keep my hands to myself. Go to sleep, before I disgrace us both."

Kate stretched and burrowed deeper into her pillow. Soon the rain and the wind and even Sean receded into nothingness, and she was dreaming dreams.

When she awakened hours later, the room was dark and cold and she was alone. For a reason she could never have explained, she turned onto her stomach, buried her head in her arms and wept with grief.

8

At dinner Kate was puffy-eyed and quiet, wishing she'd never come to Australia. Maybe she wouldn't be so deeply, hopelessly in love with Sean Harris if she'd stayed where she belonged.

Later, when the dishes were washed and dried and put away, Ellen sat down at her quilting frame and showed Kate how to work a simple stitch. While they sewed, Sean and Blue played a cutthroat game of chess. The children were sitting in front of a television set, watching a picture that intermittently faded and jiggled on the screen.

"Is that good for their eyes?" Kate asked, worried.

"They'll soon tire of it," Ellen answered with a contented sigh, and she was right. Minutes later, the TV was silent and the kids were getting out various books and toys.

Because they got up early and worked hard, the McAllisters liked to be in bed by eight. Kate, having had a long nap, was wide awake, but she didn't want to disrupt the household, so she helped herself to one of Ellen's romance novels, gave Sean an innocuous good-night kiss and went off to her room.

About a hundred pages into the book Kate realized she'd selected the wrong reading material for keeping her mind off Sean and all the sweet delights she'd known in his arms. She closed the paperback and turned out the light to stare up at the ceiling with unblinking eyes.

She tried counting sheep next, and was certain she got through the McAllisters' entire flock without missing so much as a lamb. She was still sleepless, and her body was still wanting Sean.

She turned the light back on and started to read again. This time she didn't stop until the happily-ever-after ending, and a glance at her watch told her that it was nearly dawn. Kate got out of bed and quietly got dressed.

Sean was in the kitchen, drinking instant coffee by the hearth, when she arrived there. He'd already built the fire to a crackling blaze.

"Where do they get wood?" Kate asked. She hadn't stopped to wonder before, but the land was barren for miles around.

Sean set aside his coffee and drew her into the circle of his arms as though she'd asked some romantic question. "There's an occasional stand of gum trees about," he answered, his lips a fraction of an inch from Kate's. "And they have some of it shipped in by rail, from a town about ninety-five kilometers south of here."

Kate's breasts were pressed into the hard wall of Sean's chest. "Oh," she said weakly. She was still holding the romance novel she'd read during the night in one hand, and it dropped to the floor.

Sean released her to retrieve it, and his eyes danced in the dim light of the fire as he looked at the cover and then at Kate. "Katie-did," he teased, "I'm surprised at you."

Kate was quietly defiant. "I liked it," she said, sticking out her chin. "In fact, I can't wait to buy a supply for myself."

Sean tossed the book onto the table with a chuckle and then pulled her close again, his hand grasping the waistband of her jeans. His fingers were warm against the bare skin of her abdomen, and he seemed in no hurry to withdraw.

Kate gave a trembling sigh. She was helpless where this man was concerned. "A-are we leaving today?"

Sean nodded, bending his head to nibble at her lips. "Yes, sheila. Provided the runway isn't knee-deep in mud, we're taking off after breakfast." He turned his hand to caress the nest of silk at the junction of Kate's thighs. "If we stay," he continued, answering the question Kate hadn't the breath to voice, "I'll have to take you somewhere private and have my way with you."

At the sound of footsteps on the stairs, Sean stepped back, ending the intimate embrace. Kate swayed on her feet, and he gripped her shoulders, pressing her onto one of the benches beside the table. She was trying to catch her breath when Blue came into the kitchen, whistling softly.

"Good morning," he said, his grin taking in both his guests in a single sweep. "Off to the blue sky, are you?"

"If the runway's clear," Sean answered, and he sounded as distracted as Kate felt.

Blue took the kettle from the stove and poured steaming water into a mug, adding instant coffee and sugar to that. He stooped slightly to look out the window and assess the sky. "Should be all right," he said. "Then again, you could be here for weeks."

"Now there was a conclusive statement," Sean remarked.

Blue's eyes were twinkling in the dim, cozy light of the warm kitchen. "Anxious to see the last of us, are you?" he teased. "I don't mind telling you, I'm insulted."

Sean laughed. "Who's insulted?" he returned. "You and Ellen haven't been to Sydney in six years."

While the men went on arguing good-naturedly, Kate went to the cupboard for a cup, then to the stove for hot water and coffee crystals. She stood at a far window, looking out at the sky. As she watched, streaks of gray shot through the black velvet expanse, following by tinges of crimson and apricot. The spectacle was stunning.

Sean appeared beside her. "What do you see out there, sheila?" he asked softly.

"Magic," Kate replied, glad to be next to him.

Soon the sky had performed all its tricks and the kitchen was full of noise and laughter. Kate set the table for breakfast, while Ellen prepared oatmeal, toasted bread, sausage and the ever-present eggs.

When the meal was over, Blue put on his coat and hat. Ellen and the children gathered around him in a happy ritual of hugging and kissing. Kate's throat felt thick as she watched.

After Blue had said a morning farewell to his wife and children, he shifted his eyes to Kate. "It was good to meet you, Kate Blake. Come back and see us again soon."

Kate nodded and muttered her thanks as Sean put on his own hat and coat to follow his friend outside.

Ellen was busy clearing the table, her motions too swift and intense for the simple job. It was plain to see that she already missed her husband, even though he would be back in time for supper.

"Daddy forgot his tucker!" Sarah cried suddenly, running to fetch the canvas bag that contained a hearty homemade lunch and dashing for the door.

John and Margaret ran out behind her.

Kate felt a pang at the prospect of leaving this family. She'd never seen one quite like it before, and she hadn't dreamed such simple, unadorned happiness really existed.

When Sean came back inside minutes later, he announced that the runway was dry enough for a takeoff. Kate went to gather her things, bringing her small leather suitcase downstairs with her.

The time with Ellen and Blue and their children had been precious to Kate. She hugged her new friend and said a soft goodbye.

There were bright tears in Ellen's eyes. "Don't be a stranger," she said, before turning to embrace Sean.

Kate didn't let her tears fall until she and Sean were inside the airplane and racing along the runway to meet the blue sky.

"What's wrong?" Sean asked with genuine concern in his voice as the small craft shot into the air. The landing gear made a *ker-thump* sound as it moved back into the belly of the plane.

Kate sniffled and dried her cheeks with the back of one hand. "They're so happy," she said.

"And that's something to cry about?" Sean persisted, frowning in puzzlement.

"It is if you realize you've never even *seen* that kind of happiness before, let alone had it for yourself."

Sean was quiet for a long time. When he finally spoke, they were flying at a level altitude. Far below, a small stream looked like a long mud puddle in the brown grass, and kangaroos paused to drink. "Abby thought Ellen ought to leave Blue and get herself a career in the city," he said, and his voice was flat, emotionless.

Kate supposed it was hard for him, even now, to speak of Abby. "Ellen told me," she answered. "Did Abby want a career?"

Sean made a raw sound in his throat that was probably meant to pass as a chuckle. "Definitely not. She made a life's work out of telling other people what to do."

Kate regretted bringing Abby's name up in conversation, but she knew that she and Sean had to talk about her sister. If they didn't, she would always hover over them like a ghost. "You sound as though you hated her," she said.

"Toward the end," Sean answered, "I did."

The subject was too painful; Kate had to back away. "Where did you meet Blue McAllister?"

There was relief in Sean's voice when he answered, "Flight school. He and I went to work for Austra-Air at the same time."

"And Ellen?"

"She was a buyer for a chain of department stores. They met on one of Blue's flights."

Kate was surprised. She'd pictured Blue and Ellen growing up close to the land. "How on earth did they end up way out here on a sheep station?''

''The station was Blue's dream. Ellen loved him enough to share it.''

Kate was quiet for a long time. She looked out at the raw panorama spread out below, trying to remember how it had felt to live and work in Seattle, to be mainly concerned with the course of her father's career. The whole scenario had about as much reality for her as a rerun of a TV movie.

''What's your dream, Sean?'' she finally dared to ask.

Sean had one hand on his knee, the other on the control lever. ''I want to keep on flying,'' he answered in a noncommittal tone without looking at Kate.

''There has to be more than that,'' Kate ventured.

Sean sighed, and she knew by the angle of his head that his eyes, hidden behind a pair of mirrored sunglasses, were fixed on the horizon. ''All right,'' he said, ''I'll tell you. I'd like to have a wife who looked at me the way Ellen looks at Blue.''

Kate smiled. "That shouldn't be hard to manage. I would imagine you have women falling at your feet, Captain Harris."

At last Sean spared her a glance. "Most of them are only looking for a good time," he said. "I want a woman who can say her wedding vows and mean them."

Back to Abby again. Kate let out her breath. "How about you? Did you keep your vows, Sean?"

His jawline hardened visibly. "I've never gone back on my word in my life," he replied, and Kate knew he was telling the truth. He had been faithful to Abby, even when he was desperately unhappy.

Kate reached out and rested a gentle hand on Sean's leg. "We need to talk about my sister," she said.

"Personally," Sean responded, "I'd like to forget she ever existed."

Kate was annoyed, sensing the depths of Sean's stubbornness. "What about Gil? He's a part of Abby. Do you want to forget about him, too?"

"Of course not," Sean snapped. "If it hadn't been for him, that part of my life would have been a total waste."

Kate drew a deep breath and let it out slowly. "Was it really that bad?"

He turned his head in Kate's direction, but she couldn't see his eyes because of the sunglasses he wore. "It was that bad," he answered.

"Then why didn't you divorce her?" Kate asked, exasperated.

Sean's answer stunned her. "I did," he said. "Two days after I moved out of the house, she drove her car off a cliff."

Several long moments passed before Kate could speak. Even now she was afraid to ask the question that had plagued her ever since Abby's death, but she made herself do it. "Did you take Gil away from her? Is that why she did it?"

Sean shoved splayed fingers through his dark hair. "She didn't want him," he said in a voice so low that Kate could barely hear it. "She brought him to my office that afternoon and left him with my secretary—along with a note saying she was going to meet her lover in Brisbane. They were planning to be married once the divorce went through, according to her."

Kate closed her eyes. As painful as any reminder of Abby was to her, it was a tremendous relief to know that her sister hadn't died on purpose. "Why didn't you tell us that before? My parents and I have always thought she killed herself.''

"No one seemed very interested in anything I had to say at the time," Sean answered.

It was true. Everyone had been so caught up in their own feelings and conclusions about Abby's death that very few questions were asked. "I'm sorry, Sean," Kate said softly.

Sean had evidently spotted their destination. He began guiding the small plane downward, and the conversation was clearly over.

The campsite was in the shelter of a grassy canyon, where a small, spring-fed lake was hidden away. Since they had landed a mile off, by Kate's calculations, she and Sean had to carry their supplies a considerable distance.

When several trips had been made, and Sean was satisfied that they had everything they needed, he set about putting up the tent. Kate, exhausted by the treks back and forth between the plane and camp, collapsed onto the ground.

"I wouldn't do that again if I were you," Sean commented without looking up from his task. "We get the occasional milk snake 'round here."

Kate shot back to her feet and looked frantically around. When there was no sign of a snake, she sat down again. "Next you're going to tell me there are crocodiles in the water," she said, gesturing toward the lake.

Sean's white teeth showed in a grin. "Just don't expect me to wrestle one for you, love. This isn't the movies and I'm not Paul Hogan."

Kate sniffed. "You mean, you wouldn't even try to save me?" she asked, insulted.

"I'd say it would be the croc who needed saving," he replied, going on with his work. He tossed his head, as if to shake away some dreadful image. "Poor devil," he added.

"What kind of Australian are you?" Kate grinned, folding her arms across her chest.

"The kind who can manage the likes of you," Sean responded, finishing with the tent and dusting his hands together at a job well done. "Come on," he said, taking up a tackle box and two fishing poles. "Let's go catch our supper."

"Supper?" Kate echoed. "We haven't even had lunch."

Sean dropped the fishing poles and the tackle box and came toward her, grinning. "Lunch, is it?" he teased. "Now there's an idea I can warm up to. Come here, Katie-did, and give me lunch."

Kate's cheeks were hot, and she retreated a step, unconsciously holding the buttoned front of her shirt together with one hand. She wanted

Sean as much as he wanted her—but she wanted him *later*, in the privacy of the tent. "I think we should go fishing after all," she said formally.

Sean was still advancing. Then, suddenly, he stopped in his tracks. A look of absolute horror contorted his features, and he yelled, "Look out!"

Kate sprang into his arms, her heart hammering against her breastbone, only to find that he was laughing. A wild turn of her head showed her that there was nothing behind her. "Bastard," she said, doubling up her fists and slamming them against Sean's chest.

He caught her by the waistband of her jeans, opening the snap with a motion of his thumb. A slight pull made the zipper come undone. "You were awake all night, wanting me," he said in a low, hoarse voice.

It was true, and Kate couldn't deny it, much as she wanted to. "How do you know?" she threw out lamely.

Sean's hand slid up under her shirt, over her rib cage to the rounded underside of her breast. "It was a wild guess," he replied, and a grin spread across his tanned face as Kate flinched at the passing of a fingertip over her nipple.

"S-someone might see us," Kate managed. As much as she longed for and needed this man, something deep inside her always wanted to erect a barrier. She needed a place to hide.

"Only the 'roos and the snakes," Sean answered with an easy shrug. He was unbuttoning Kate's shirt now, and there was nothing she could do to stop him. Her hands hung uselessly at her sides.

"We c-could go inside the tent," she suggested.

Sean shook his head. "I want to have you in the bright light of day, Katie-did," he answered.

A tremor went through Kate as he slid her flannel shirt off over her shoulders and arms and tossed it onto the grass. Her full breasts swelled against the scanty cloth of her undershirt, straining to be free.

He squatted to untie and remove her boots, then peeled away her stockings. The feel of his hands on her bare feet was so unexpectedly erotic that she shivered. He claimed her jeans and panties next, leaving the undershirt for last. After he'd pulled it ever so slowly over her head, Kate stood naked before him.

She felt no more shame than Eve had before the fall from grace.

"My God, you're beautiful," Sean whispered, his hands resting lightly, almost reverently, on the curves of Kate's hips.

Kate reached back to undo her French braid, delighted by the catch in Sean's breathing as her bare breasts rose. Then she shook her head until her hair lay about her shoulders. In those moments it was easy to believe that she was the only woman on earth, and Sean the only man.

He took off his hat first, tossing it into the grass. Then he removed his shirt. Goose bumps appeared on his skin as the cool breeze touched him, but Kate doubted that he felt the cold any more than she did.

She stepped forward to unfasten his belt and open his jeans. Sean groaned and let his head fall back when she clasped him boldly in one hand, taking his measure with long, gliding strokes of her palm.

He dug his fingers into her bare shoulders as he dragged her close and propelled her into a hard, elemental kiss. When it was over, Kate ached to possess and be possessed. Her body had long since made itself ready for Sean.

"I need you so much," she whispered. "Please don't make me wait this time."

Sean uttered a hoarse chuckle. "I don't think I could manage that," he admitted. Then, in a motion that dated back to Adam, he clasped Kate by the waist and lifted her to the top of his shaft.

She drew in her breath as she felt him nudging the portal of her womanhood, and it came out as a ragged rendering of his name.

He lowered her slowly, begrudging every fraction of an inch she gained, making her pay for it with pleas and promises. By the time she'd taken all of him, she was delirious with need.

Kate shivered as he unsheathed himself rapidly, then began the sweet process of entering her again. "Oh, Sean," she whispered, "please."

But he stopped and tilted her back, only partly joined with him, so that he could take one of her nipples into his mouth. A jolt of pleasure went through Kate at this new contact, and she thrust herself down upon him in response, taking matters into her own hands.

Sean groaned and lifted her again, slowly, slowly, all the while feeding greedily at her breast.

She wrapped one arm around his neck and entangled her free hand in his hair, whispering his name over and over again as a litany and a plea.

Finally Sean reached the limits of his control. He dropped to his knees in the grass without ever breaking contact with Kate, and allowed her her freedom. She began to rise and fall and writhe upon him, her body taking over her entire being while her mind spun in another universe.

When Kate cried out in unbearable pleasure, Sean thrust her bountiful breasts together with his hands and ran his tongue back and forth across the nipples. Kate gave cry after primitive cry while her body bucked spasmodically in release.

She was still in a daze when Sean's moment came. He stiffened violently beneath her and then thrust his hips upward, spilling himself into her.

She prayed silently that he had given her a child, so that she would have something left of him when the inevitable happened and they parted. All her dreams and fears entangled with one another and Kate dropped her head to Sean's bare shoulder and sobbed.

He was still breathing too hard to speak, but his hands roved soothingly over the naked skin of her back and buttocks, and his lips moved against her temple. "What is it, sheila?" he asked softly when he could speak. His hand was under Kate's chin then, and he was looking deep into her eyes.

Kate couldn't speak of parting, not when she and Sean were still joined together. She simply couldn't. She shook her head wildly and pressed her wet cheek against his shoulder. The ghosts of people she'd trusted—Abby, Brad, her father— were all around, taunting her. "Hold me," she said.

He reached out and found his shirt, which he draped gently over Kate's trembling shoulders, and then he put his arms around her. "I love you," he told her.

For a moment Kate couldn't believe she'd heard the words. "What?" she sniffed.

He chuckled, holding her even more tightly. "I said I love you," he answered.

Kate drew back far enough to search his face and the depths of his green, green eyes. "You do?" she marveled.

Sean sighed in a put-upon way. "That isn't the customary response to such a declaration, Katie-did," he pointed out. "Do you love me or not?"

Kate pretended to consider the question. "I love you," she professed in the tone of one making a sudden decision. Then she couldn't tease any longer. "I always have," she added softly.

He kissed her, deeply and thoroughly, and she could feel him stirring inside her. He slipped his hands beneath the shirt and around her rib cage, rising unerringly to her breasts. "Marry me," he said when the kiss ended.

Kate was dizzy, and she could barely see for the stars in her eyes. "Anytime," she answered.

Sean opened the shirt and lifted her breasts in both his hands. "I'll be a demanding husband," he warned, chafing sensitive nipples with the pads of his thumbs. He was getting harder inside her.

"I'll be a demanding wife," Kate answered, giving a small sigh as she began to move upon Sean.

He stopped her movements to prolong the delicious friction. Nibbling at her ear, he said, "I'll want you often."

"Good," Kate breathed, writhing slightly.

Sean groaned at the sensation this produced, then pressed Kate backward into the grass. The fabric of his shirt protected her from the chill of the ground as he withdrew and then drove into her, and she bent her knees in order to receive him.

Satisfaction came to Kate first, so she had the special pleasure of guiding Sean through his. She ran her hands up and down the smooth flesh of his back and whispered soft, soothing words as he fought against the inevitable and then succumbed.

He fell to Kate when it was over, gasping and exhausted, and still she held him. Presently he rolled onto his side, drawing Kate close as he moved. He kissed the top of her head and squeezed her tightly.

"I hope I'm pregnant," she said dreamily.

Sean sat bolt upright and stared down at her. "What?" he rasped.

"I said—"

"I know what you said, damn it!" Sean growled. Then he swore roundly, got to his feet and fastened his jeans.

Kate stared up at him, startled and scared. "Sean—"

"I thought you were protected," he said.

It was like being slapped. "You thought..." She snatched up her clothes and began scrambling back into them. "Damn you, Sean Harris!" she screamed.

He turned away, shoving one hand through his hair. "I won't be able to bear it if you leave carrying a child," he said in a voice so low that Kate barely heard him.

Her eyes were hot with tears—tears of relief and confusion and love. She went around to face him, snapping her jeans as she moved, then pulling her undershirt into place. "Sean, I don't have any plans to leave."

He looked at her with mingled hope and contempt. "You will, love," he said. "As soon as your beloved daddy crooks his finger, you'll be on a plane home."

Kate had to vent her frustration somehow, so she stomped one foot. "I'll give you a *finger*, you officious creep!" she yelled, holding up the pertinent digit.

Sean laughed in spite of himself. "God, but you do need taming, sheila," he said.

Kate kicked dirt at him with her bare foot. "You go to hell!" she shouted, still furious over his remark about her allegiance to her father. Deep down inside, she was terribly afraid he might be right.

"Come here," Sean ordered quietly.

"Drop dead," Kate answered, storming off in the direction of the plane. In that moment she would have given her soul for a pilot's license.

Not to mention her boots.

9

Midway between the campsite and Sean's plane, Kate stepped on a thistle and began hopping about awkwardly on one foot in a ceremony of pain.

Sean made an affectionately contemptuous sound as he lifted her into his arms to carry her back to the camp. "You're lucky I don't believe in hitting women," he said with a philosophical air about him. "If I did, I'd turn you over my knee right now and blister your delectable little rear end."

Kate glared at him. "Put me down," she said.

"It'll hurt if I do," Sean warned.

The thistle in Kate's foot was already stinging. "Then don't," she conceded grudgingly.

Sean chuckled and set her carefully on a large stone near the tent. Then, squatting down in front of her, he lifted her wounded foot and examined it with a frown. "Nasty bit of business, that," he commented. "Next time you stomp off in a rage, sheila, wear your boots."

"Don't patronize me," Kate hissed, squeezing her eyes shut when she saw that Sean was about to remove the thistle. There was a biting sting and then relief.

Sean set her wounded foot on her knee. "There's still the iodine," he said, rummaging around in one of the packs they'd brought.

Kate figured the medicine would hurt worse than the injury, and she was right. Tears burned in her eyes when Sean applied the iodine, and her teeth sank into her lower lip.

Gripping her foot in a gentle grasp, Sean put a Band-Aid over the wound and followed that with a light kiss.

Kate braced herself. "Would it really be so terrible if I had your baby?" she asked.

Sean handed Kate her stockings, then her hiking boots. "It would if you got on a plane and went back to the States," he answered, looking not at her but at the sparkling waters of the hidden lake. "I won't have my children living on different continents."

"You asked me to marry you a little while ago," Kate reminded him. "Did you mean it?"

Sean got to his feet. The winter sun was at his back, casting a golden aura all around him. "I meant it," he said. "But there won't be any babies until we're sure it's going to work out."

"That's the stupidest thing I've ever heard," Kate argued, lacing up one of her boots. "If you don't think we can make it, why the hell did you bother to propose?"

Sean cupped his hand under her chin and made her look up at his face. "Because I love you, and I need you," he said forthrightly.

"Well, then," Kate pressed, standing.

"I felt the same way about Abby," he answered tightly. Then he took up the fishing poles and the tackle box again, and he walked away.

Kate still didn't know whether he'd really meant his marriage proposal. It had seemed so, but then he'd made that ominous remark about Abby. She followed him down to the rocky bank of the lake and took one of the fishing poles when he set them down. "I guess you don't trust me much," she observed.

Sean took a jar of fish eggs from the tackle box, opened it and baited his hook. "I think we should live together for a while," he announced.

"No way," said Kate, thinking of Gil as well as herself and Sean. "If you don't have enough confidence in what we have together to marry me, then we're better off to stay on separate continents."

Sean handed Kate the pole with the baited hook. "What do we have, Katie-did? Besides the sexual thing, I mean?"

Kate cast her hook into the water and reeled in the slack in her line. "I don't know. But if it's what I saw back there at the McAllisters', I want a shot at it."

Sean looked at her and grinned. "Me, too," he answered.

They fished in silence for a while, neither getting so much as a bite, and then Sean said, "I've got a flight to Hong Kong day after tomorrow. Come with me."

Kate hesitated. "I don't think so."

"Why not?"

"Because I want to spend some time with Gil, for one thing. And I need to think about what's happening between you and me. In case you haven't noticed, Sean Harris, it's hard for me to put one sensible thought in front of another when you're around."

He grinned. "I have the same problem."

Kate drew a deep breath. Since they were talking calmly, now seemed as good a time as any to broach the subject of taking Gil back to America for a visit with his maternal grandparents. "Mother and Daddy would love to see Gil," she ventured.

Sean stiffened slightly. "Fine. Let them fly down here."

Kate sighed. "Sean, my father is getting older, and he's not in the best of health. I think the trip might be too much for him."

Sean was quiet for a long time. Out of the corner of her eye, Kate could see that his jawline was as hard as the volcanic rock embedded in the walls of the canyon rising around the lake. "I don't trust him," he said finally.

Kate gave her line a few tugs, hoping to interest a fish. "Okay," she answered, "but it's only fair to tell you that if we get married, I plan to make regular trips back to the States. And if we have a child, I'm taking him or her with me."

Sean's resentment was almost tangible. "Fine," he said. "Let's just forget about having babies and getting married. That will make everything simple."

"Damn," Kate muttered through her teeth. "What did my father do to make you hate him so much?"

"He tried to steal my son."

Kate's pole trembled in her hands. "I know you think Daddy was behind that, Sean, but you're wrong. He would never do a thing like that."

"A month ago you would have told me that what's-his-name wouldn't sell cocaine," Sean pointed out, reeling in his line with a furious motion of his hand and then casting it again.

The reminder of Brad shook Kate's confidence in her own instincts. She *had* trusted her fiancé with her whole heart, and she'd been so terribly wrong. She bit into her lower lip and said nothing, and her pole and the lake blurred into each other.

Sean finally put his hand on hers. "Kate, I'm sorry," he said. "I shouldn't have thrown that in your face."

Kate couldn't look at him. "No. You were right—I trusted Brad. I would have married him."

"Kate."

"What's your secret, Sean?" she asked miserably, still avoiding his eyes. "What terrible thing am I going to find out about you now that I'm so much in love with you that there's no going back?''

He took her pole and set it aside with his own. "I've never lied to you about anything, Kate, and I don't plan to start." He spread his hands. "I'm just what I represent myself to be—a man who loves you."

Kate went into his arms and held on tight to his waist. "If this falls through," she whispered, "I won't be able to stand it."

Sean entangled his fingers gently in her hair and drew her head back to make her look at him. "I'm not going to betray you, Kate," he promised hoarsely.

She gazed into his eyes, letting all her fears and insecurities show. There was no hiding from this man who could turn her mind and body inside out at will. "I'll marry you, if you still want me," she said softly. "As soon as you get back from Hong Kong, we'll arrange for the license."

Sean nodded. "It's a deal, Yank," he said with a grin.

Kate put her arms around his neck and kissed him. "There's one other thing, Sean," she said after a long time. "I can't live in Abby's house."

"Fair enough," he answered. "We'll shop for one of our own after the honeymoon."

Kate was silent a moment, gathering courage for what she wanted to suggest. "We could take Gil with us," she said cautiously.

"On our honeymoon? Not likely, sheila."

Kate forged bravely ahead as though he hadn't spoken. "It's summer in the States," she said. "Gil would love Seattle, and on our way home, we could take him to Disneyland."

Sean's face hardened. "Is that what this is all about? You want to get married so your parents can get a look at Gil?"

"Of course not!" Kate protested, insulted.

He smiled, but the expression wasn't pleasant. "Maybe they'd like to come down for the wedding," he suggested. "I'm sure they'll be pleased to learn that The Fiend has started in on their second daughter after using up their first."

"That's a terrible thing to say!" Kate cried.

"The truth is the truth, Kate," Sean said stubbornly. "When your parents find out I'm back in the family, all hell's going to break loose. You might just have to choose between them and me."

The thought was appalling—and all too possible. "Is that what you wanted Abby to do? Choose between you and them?"

Sean threw down his fishing pole without even bothering to reel in the line. "No!" he shouted. "Damn it all to hell, no!"

Kate put her pole down carefully, just to show him that some people in this world were civilized and could control their temper. With her chin high and her shoulders back, she turned and walked toward the camp.

Sean strode after her, grabbing her by the shoulders and wrenching her around. "I never asked anything of Abby but love and loyalty," he rasped. "She repaid me by getting rid of our baby and taking a lover. *Don't you ever* accuse me of trying to hurt her in any way, because I gave her everything I had!"

With that, Sean abruptly released Kate and walked away, leaving her to stand alone by the lake, staring after him. He disappeared around the canyon wall without once looking back.

Kate's emotions were in such a dither that she couldn't stand still. Her mind rang with words she wanted to forget—*She repaid me by getting rid of our baby and taking a lover.*

The solution, she knew, was to get so caught up in some task that she didn't have time to think. She busied herself gathering rocks to make a circle around the place where the bonfire would be, as she'd seen people do in the movies. After that, she gathered what stray pieces of brush she could find and piled them inside the ring of stone.

An hour passed and there was still no sign of Sean.

Kate dragged a box of canned goods over near the nonexistent fire and sat down to wait, her chin in one hand. Sean would be back, she told herself. He couldn't stay away forever.

She began to tap one foot against the ground. One thing was clear—marrying Sean Harris in the near future was out of the question. He wasn't emotionally ready for such a commitment, and neither was she.

An overwhelming sadness overtook Kate, and she sighed beneath the weight of it. When they got back to Sydney, she would pack her things and return to the hotel. Once she'd had a few days to get to know Gil, she would get on a plane, go home and try to pick up the scattered pieces of her life.

The trouble was, none of them fit anymore. She was no longer Brad's fiancé or her father's press secretary, and that left her with nothing to be. She was shamed anew by the realization that, for all her efforts, she'd never built a life for herself.

Kate was chewing listlessly on a cold piece of Mrs. Manchester's meat pie when Sean finally returned to camp. He looked at Kate's attempt at a fire and grinned.

"What's so funny?" Kate demanded. She was through putting up with his patronizing manner.

Sean dumped an armload of dry, broken branches beside the carefully arranged rocks. He ignored Kate's question and squatted down to go through the supplies for a meat pie of his own.

"Don't you have anything to say?" she asked when the silence stretched to interminable lengths.

Sean looked up at her, chewing. "Yes," he answered. "Can you cook?"

Kate gave a strangled cry of fury and kicked dirt at him. "No, and I don't intend to learn," she said, "so you can just forget any ideas you might have of getting me to fetch and carry for you!"

"Fine," Sean told her calmly.

"Furthermore, I have no intention of marrying anybody with a temper like yours."

"Good," Sean replied, serenely consuming the rest of his meat pie.

Kate sank to her knees beside him and shoved one hand through her hair. "Aren't you going to ask me to forgive you for deserting me like that?" she asked.

"No," Sean answered. "I'm not."

"You're not sorry?"

Sean shook his head. "It was leave or wring your neck, sheila. I'm still not sure I made the right choice."

Regally Kate got to her feet, marched over to the tent and crawled inside. Then she summarily zipped the zipper.

A marriage to Sean would never work out anyway, she assured herself. And then she lay down on the sleeping bag she was going to have to share with him that night and cried until her nose was red.

Some time later the zipper on the tent made a rasping sound as Sean opened it. He crawled in to lie beside Kate, gathering her into his arms. "Don't cry, sheila," he whispered, holding her close.

Kate slipped her arms around his neck; she couldn't help it. "We're hopeless," she said.

He chuckled. "No. Where there's this much love, there's always hope. But you were right before." He paused and sighed. "We need time to think this through, both of us."

For all the reassurance in his words, there was a note of resignation, too, and Kate was anything but comforted. She couldn't pretend that nothing was wrong, either, because something was. "What did you mean when you said Abby got rid of your baby?" she asked, her voice barely more than a whisper.

Sean didn't put her away from him, but his arms didn't hold her quite so tightly. "Exactly what you think I meant," he answered after a long time.

Kate closed her eyes. "I'm sorry, Sean."

"So am I, but it's over and done. It's a mistake for us to talk about Abby. We're both scared, and we keep dragging her memory out and throwing it between us."

Kate knew he was right, but she wasn't sure they'd ever be able to make a relationship work. Sure, they had passion, but Sean and Abby had probably had that in the beginning, too. Would their lovers' quarrels become vicious battles at some point in the future?

Kate couldn't bear the thought. "Make love to me, Sean," she whispered, desperate for some distraction from her confusion.

He laughed, but the sound had elements of a hoarse sob. "There's a request I'll never refuse, Katie-did," he said. But instead of kissing her, or opening her shirt or jeans, he caught her by one hand and hauled her out of the tent.

"I think you may be an exhibitionist at heart," she commented, disgruntled, and Sean laughed again.

He kept right on walking toward the lake, though, pulling Kate after him.

When he finally let go of her hand, he immediately tossed aside his hat, then kicked off his boots. His socks, jeans and shirt soon followed.

Kate looked at the water with concern. "Are there snakes or crocodiles in there?" she asked.

"Probably not," Sean answered, wading into the water.

He was as magnificent naked as he was dressed, and Kate couldn't help staring at him. "Come back here," she said lamely.

Sean grinned. "Come and get me," he challenged.

"Damn it, it's winter," Kate pointed out, hugging herself.

"Chicken," he replied.

His insolence made Kate get out of her boots and her clothes and stomp furiously into the water that could be infested with creatures she wouldn't even recognize. When she stood face-to-face with Sean, he chuckled at her angry expression and began to bathe her.

The water was cold, but Kate was transfixed by the gentle splashing motions of Sean's hands. He washed her face, her shoulders, her back and breasts and beneath her arms, and it was a strangely sensual experience.

When he proceeded to the lower part of her body, her breath caught in her lungs and the already taut tips of her breasts grew tighter still. She ran her tongue over her lips as he parted her, cried out when he claimed her with a sudden thrust of his fingers.

"Easy," he said, as the water began to churn around them from the frantic motions of Kate's hips. "Take it slow and easy, sheila."

"I—oh, God—I can't!" Kate cried. His thumb was moving around and around on her, making her slippery even though she was waist-deep in water. "Oh, Sean . . ."

He bent to take one of her nipples into his mouth, and Kate clutched at him, driven by a need she hadn't been prepared for. Her nails left pink curves in the flesh of his shoulders, but she didn't care. She moved wildly in the water, seeking him.

"Take me," she pleaded.

"Later," he replied. "Right now I want to see your pleasure, Kate. I want to watch you respond to me."

"Oh," she whispered, *"oh..."*

Sean intensified his efforts, greedy at her breasts, a merciless conqueror. When she stiffened violently and cried out in relief, she knew he was watching her every reaction, and that made her gratification even keener.

When the water was still at last, he kissed her and maneuvered her gently onto his shaft. Soon the lake was wild again, and the cries that filled the air were Sean's.

They didn't dress immediately, but dried each other and crept into the tent to lie entwined in sweet silence and sleep. When Kate awakened, Sean was outside, whistling, and she could hear the cheery crackle of a campfire.

Hastily Kate found the clothes Sean had left for her and put them on. When she crawled out of the tent, he was squatting beside the fire, stirring something in a frying pan, and dusk was deepening the shadows that sprawled across the lake.

"What's that?" Kate asked, sniffing.

Sean grinned at her. "No worries, love. It's nothing on the endangered species list."

"Don't tease me," Kate fussed, going to sit near him on the ground. "I just woke up."

He treated her to a brief, smacking kiss but said nothing.

Looking at him, she wondered how she was going to live without him—for a few days or for a lifetime. "Do you absolutely have to go to Hong Kong?" she asked.

"Yes," he answered. "You can still come with me, you know."

She shook her head. "There will be other trips," she said, hoping against hope that what she was saying was true. "Right now I need some time and space, and so do you."

Sean only shrugged and went back to his cooking. It looked to Kate like some kind of chops, and it smelled wonderful. Her stomach grumbled.

Sean chuckled. "Hungry, sheila?"

Kate nodded, licking her lips.

"Strange thing about love," Sean philoso-phized. "It either takes your appetite away com-pletely or makes you eat like a crazed shark." He reached out to give the contents of another ket-tle a knowledgeable shake. "I probably shouldn't give you any dinner, since you refuse to do your share of the cooking."

Kate found metal plates and utensils for them both. "Does setting the table count?" she asked.

"That depends," Sean said, pausing to look at Kate's chest. Her buttons were open, and she was straining against the undershirt.

"On what?" she breathed.

Sean reached over and lowered the under-shirt, revealing both her breasts. He bent and kissed each nipple lightly. "On whether or not you're willing to provide dessert," he replied.

Kate held a breast for him with one hand and entangled the other in his hair. "Does this an-swer your question?" she asked, her voice husky with pleasure.

He suckled for a few moments, then withdrew and righted her undershirt. "Absolutely," he answered belatedly.

The mosquitoes were thick that night, so they retired to the tent after their meal. Kate couldn't see a thing in the darkness, but she could hear

Sean undressing as she took off her outer clothes. She was kneeling, clad only in her panties and undershirt, when he reached out for her.

"What do you want, Kate?" she heard him ask in a low, raspy voice. He was close; his hands were resting on her bare thighs and she could catch the clean scent of him.

Kate drew her undershirt off over her head and then took his hands in hers. For an answer, she laid his palms against her swollen breasts. Her nipples hardened.

Sean caressed her for a while, then gently turned her so that her back was to him. He moved one of his hands between one breast and then the other, fondling them in turn, while he moved his other lightly over her belly.

Kate's breathing was quick and shallow, and despite the chill of the night, she was so warm that she was perspiring lightly. She squirmed backward until she found what she wanted and needed, and she took it.

Sean had not expected to be taken prisoner, and he gave a sharp gasp of pleasure.

Bracing herself against the tent floor with her hands, Kate allowed her instincts free reign and became the conqueror. Sean groaned helplessly as she had her relentless way with him, now teasing, now tempting, now taking him in earnest.

He gave up what Kate took from him with a defiant, adoring shout, then turned her and pressed her to the sleeping bag. She still could not see him, but she could feel the caresses of his hands and the touch of his lips, and that was enough.

"You'll have to give an accounting for that, sheila," he promised between deep, ragged breaths. He found her with his strong fingers and began a rhythmic, circular massage that soon had Kate writhing, her hands stretched above her head.

Sean found them and imprisoned them in his fist, holding them where they were. Kate's back arched, and a whimper escaped her as he continued to soothe and torment her at once.

"I love you," she managed as he worked her skillfully toward frenzy. "Oh, God, I love you so much."

"Then stay with me," he answered, showing her no more mercy than she had shown him. "You belong with me, Kate—in my house and my bed."

She moaned.

He took her to the east and west and north and south of heaven itself before allowing her a slow descent to earth.

In the morning they rose early to fish. It was their last day alone together, and that gave everything they did a note of sad festivity.

After lunching on their catch, they took down the tent, packed up their gear and hauled the lot of it to the airplane, where Sean stowed it neatly away. Looking back, Kate could see only a ring of stones surrounding a dead fire to mark their passing. Except for that, the ancient land was undisturbed; they might never have been there, loving and living, laughing and crying, shouting and whispering.

"We'll be back someday," Sean assured her, lifting her chin and planting a soft kiss on her mouth.

Kate nodded and turned her face toward the future, half excited and half afraid.

The small plane left the land with a roar that scattered birds and sent kangaroos hopping wildly toward the horizon. A magical time in Kate's life was ending, and she knew it, and she wanted to cling to it with both hands.

Of course, there was no way to do that.

They landed once, around noon, at an isolated place that sold hamburgers and gasoline to truckers and pilots, and took off again immediately.

"I didn't bring you out here to make you sad, Kate," Sean remarked, having caught the forlorn expression on her face.

She nodded, her hands clenched together in her lap. "I know," she said. How could she explain the feeling of loss she had, and the sense that it would be permanent?

They landed at the small airport outside of Sydney a few hours later, and neither of them spoke as they carried their gear from the plane to the waiting Jeep. Sean had a word with a mechanic, and then they were off.

"I'm moving back to the hotel," Kate said, uttering her first sentence in over an hour.

"Tonight?" Sean asked. There was no challenge or recrimination in his voice.

"Yes."

"Why?"

"Because of Gil. Because of Abby," Kate whispered. "Because we can't be in the same house together without ending up in each other's arms."

Sean shrugged and took Kate to the hotel where she'd stayed her first night in Sydney. He waited until she'd booked a room, then kissed her lightly on the cheek and left.

An hour later her suitcases arrived by cab. She was on the telephone when the bellhop brought them up, but she managed to tip him and wave her thanks without interrupting the call.

"So," she said when the door had closed behind the young man. "What would you and Daddy think if I married Sean Harris?"

Her mother's stunned silence was answer enough.

10

"How long will you be in Hong Kong?" Kate asked, holding the telephone receiver to her ear with one hand and towel-drying her freshly shampooed hair with the other.

"Three or four days," Sean answered. He sounded as glum as Kate felt. "You might as well come here and stay, since I'll be gone."

She smiled. "That was a very transparent attempt to get me to feel sorry for you," she said.

He chuckled ruefully. "Did it work?"

"Yes," Kate answered, "but I'm still staying here."

"Have it your way, sheila."

Kate drew a deep, weary breath. "I would like to spend some time with Gil, if that's all right with you."

"It's fine. Listen, love, I'm not very good at small talk. Will you have dinner with me tonight?"

"No," Kate answered, remembering the chops he'd cooked by the campfire. "I had dinner with you last night. I'll see you when you get back from the Orient."

Sean sighed. "Good night, Kate."

"Good night," she responded gently before hanging up.

The evening news was flickering on the television screen, so Kate went over and turned up the sound. As events happening overseas were recapped by a brisk Australian voice, a picture of her father's face filled the screen. He was standing behind the president's desk, witnessing the signing of an important bill he'd been trying to push through the Senate for months, and he looked justifiably proud of his accomplishment.

Kate felt a certain homesickness, then cinched the belt of her heavy terry cloth robe a little tighter and sat down on the edge of her bed to eat a supper brought to her by room service. As much as she loved Sean and Gil, it was going to be difficult to live so far from friends and family.

When a silly game show came on, she got up to turn off the TV. She thought of Abby, and wondered how many of her sister's problems could have been solved by an extended visit home.

In a moment, Kate's sister and mother were both inside her head, yammering that it would be a mistake to marry Sean. She shut them up by turning the game show back on.

Kate slept in the next morning, then spent a few leisurely hours shopping. She and Sean weren't planning a formal wedding, but she wanted a special dress just the same.

It was midafternoon when she arrived at Sean's house to see Gil. He and his dog, Snidely, were playing with a Frisbee on the front walk, and his eyes lit up when he saw Kate.

"Is it true?" he demanded, racing toward her but stopping just short of a hug.

"Is what true?" Kate laughed, resisting an urge to ruffle his hair. She knew that some children resented gestures like that, and she wanted very much for Gil to like her.

"Dad said you and he have been talking about getting married," Gil told her, and he looked genuinely pleased by the prospect. "Are you going to be my mom?"

So Sean had said they'd *talked* about getting married, not that they definitely would. Kate put an arm around Gil's shoulders, and they pro-

ceeded up the walk. The driver of the taxi she
had arrived in honked his horn as he drove away,
but she barely heard the sound. She was too busy
searching her mind for the proper answer to Gil's
question. "I'd be your stepmother," she said at
last. "And your aunt. But my sister was your
mom, and nothing is ever going to change that."

Worried brown eyes scanned her face. "You
wouldn't make me give Snidely away, would
you?"

"Of course not," Kate answered quickly. They
had reached the steps of the porch, and they sat
down side by side at the top. "I think Snidely is
a nice dog."

Gil was happy again. "Thanks," he said.

Kate wanted to kiss his forehead or his cheek,
but checked herself. He'd probably hate that,
think it was corny. "Say, handsome," she said as
though struck by sudden inspiration, "how
about having dinner with me tonight, since your
dad's away? We'll go wherever you like."

The child nodded eagerly. "McDonald's!"

Kate laughed and slapped her hands against
her blue-jeaned thighs. "McDonald's it is, then,
but we'd better tell Mrs. Manchester before she
goes to any trouble making you dinner."

The two went inside and found the older woman in the kitchen, rolling out dough.

"Aunt Kate's taking me to McDonald's," Gil announced importantly, "so you don't have to cook."

Mrs. Manchester smiled. "Well, that's good news," she said with enthusiasm to match Gil's. "I'll just watch the telly, then, and have something simple for supper."

"We could bring you a hamburger," Gil volunteered.

Mrs. Manchester glanced at Kate, her eyes twinkling. "I don't think that will be necessary," she said. "You just go and have a good time, young man, and don't worry about me."

Kate told the housekeeper when she would bring the boy back and called another taxi while Gil dashed upstairs to change his clothes.

"I wish you'd come back and live at our house," Gil told her when they were riding toward the nearest McDonald's in the back seat of a green cab.

Kate thought of the plans she and Sean had made to buy another house, one where Abby's memory wouldn't haunt them at every turn. "I think we might end up living together at some point," she said cautiously. "Maybe you wouldn't like it, having another person around when you're used to just your dad and Mrs. Manchester."

Shyly Gil moved a little closer to Kate on the seat. "I'd like it," he assured her in a quiet voice.

Kate was so moved that her throat thickened and, for a minute, she didn't dare look at her nephew for fear of bursting into sentimental tears. "Have you ever thought about visiting America?" she asked when she'd recovered herself.

Gil considered for a long time. "Dad says the place is overrated," he told her finally. "But I'd like to see it for myself—especially Disneyland."

Kate smiled at that. "Disneyland is one place that's everything it's cracked up to be," she told Gil.

He looked concerned. "Disneyland is cracked up? What happened to it?"

Kate laughed. "We seem to have a language barrier here. When an American says something is everything it's cracked up to be, that means it's all that you'd expect of it and more. Disneyland is wonderful."

"Oh," Gil replied, and his expression betrayed both puzzlement and relief. "That's good."

Once they'd reached McDonald's and were happily consuming their hamburgers, french fries and milk shakes, they exchanged idioms and tried to guess at their meanings. This made them both laugh so hard that people turned to look at them.

Kate would have liked to spend more time with Gil, but it was getting late and he had school in the morning. The day after that, however, would be Saturday, and Sean wasn't returning until Sunday.

"Do you have plans for this weekend?" she asked.

Gil's eyes were bright with anticipation as he shook his head.

"Then how about going to the Taronga Zoo with me? It's been a while since I've seen a platypus or a wombat or even a koala."

Gil liked the idea immediately, and he recounted the school field trip he'd just been on all the way home in the cab. Kate had the driver wait while she saw her nephew safely inside the house and said good-night.

When she got back to her hotel room, a bouquet of twelve yellow roses was waiting on her nightstand. The card read simply, ''Now and always. Love Sean.''

Kate bent to sniff the luscious scent of the flowers, feeling optimistic about all the problems and differences she and Sean would have to work out in order to make a life together. Didn't all couples have to do that?

She took a long, hot bath, read a third of the thick romance novel she'd bought that afternoon while shopping for her dress and fell into a sound sleep.

Since she hadn't found a dress she liked the day before, she went out shopping again after breakfast. At a pricey little boutique tucked away between a pawnshop and a bookstore, she found a lovely ivory silk gown with a trimming of narrow lace around the hemline and along the V-shaped bodice. It was perfect.

After paying for the dress, Kate took it back to her hotel room and hung it carefully in the closet. She was just turning away from doing that when the telephone rang.

She answered with a questioning, ''Hello?''

Sean's voice came over the wire as clear as if he were in the next room instead of on another continent. "Hello, sheila," he said. "Did you get the flowers?"

"Yes," she answered, smiling. "They're beautiful—thank you."

"I'll have to exact a certain price for them, of course," Sean teased.

Kate felt warm all over, and she wished he could be right there in that room with her. "Of course," she retorted in a low, sultry voice.

"How's Gil?" was his next question.

"He's just fine. We went to McDonald's for supper last night, and we're off to the zoo tomorrow."

"Sounds like he's pretty comfortable with you."

Kate smiled. "He asked me if I was going to be his mom."

The warmth seemed to fade from Sean's voice, at least for the moment. "What did you tell him?"

Kate sat down, feeling deflated. "I said I'd be his stepmother, *if* you and I were to get married."

"I see." Sean still sounded uncomfortable, but that awful chill was gone from his voice.

Kate was never sure where her next question came from, because she hadn't given it a moment's thought beforehand. "I don't suppose you'd let me adopt him?"

There was a long silence.

"Sean?"

"That would give you the same legal rights that Abby had," Sean reflected.

"I know," Kate answered. She knew she was walking on thin ice emotionally, and she was practically holding her breath.

"We'll talk about it when I get back," Sean said abruptly. Kate wished she could look into his eyes, for then she'd be able to read his thoughts.

"Which will be Sunday?" Kate asked brightly, anxious to soothe him.

"Probably," Sean replied. "I love you, Kate."

"And I love you."

A few moments later they hung up.

The telephone immediately jangled again, and when Kate answered, she was surprised and a little alarmed to hear the operator say, "You have another overseas call, Ms. Blake. This one is from the States."

"Thank you," Kate said, and bit down on her lip as she waited. She felt inexplicably nervous.

"Your mother tells me you're thinking of marrying that Australian," Senator Blake boomed, without so much as saying hello to his daughter first. "Don't you think that's a little idiotic, given what he did to your sister?"

Kate braced herself. "He didn't do anything to Abby. She manufactured her own set of problems, just like the rest of us."

"He'd like to have you believe that. Katherine, I want you to get on the next plane and come home. I need you here in Washington, anyway."

"I'm not going anywhere," Kate answered flatly.

She could feel the storm brewing in and around her father. "Katherine," he said in an ominously quiet voice, "I expect to see you in this office within seventy-two hours. Is that clear?"

She sighed. "I'm sorry, Daddy. I'm staying here, and I'm marrying Sean."

"If you do, by God, I'll disinherit you. You'll be left with nothing but your grandmother's trust fund!"

Kate didn't care about the money she wouldn't inherit, and her trust fund was quite adequate to her needs. But she did care about losing the senator's love and approval. "Do whatever you have to do. I've made my decision, Daddy."

At that, the senator hung up on his daughter with a resounding crash.

* * *

Kate was still upset the next morning when she set out to pick up Gil at Sean's house. Her father had no right to behave like such a tyrant, and she was going to tell him so the next time she saw him.

Gil greeted her at the front door, dressed for a day at the zoo. His smile seemed as wide as the distance between Kate and the senator. Once she was inside, the little boy gave her a shy hug. "I've been thinking about going to the States," he told her. "I think I should, since I'm half-Yankee."

Kate grinned. "I think you should, too, but your dad might have a different opinion."

"I could go if he changed his mind, though," Gil told her enthusiastically. He brought a passport from the pocket of his jacket. "See?"

Kate nodded. "You'd better put that away before you lose it or something," she said.

She was distracted from Gil by Snidely's unmistakable bark. "You get out of my kitchen, you great hulking beast!" Mrs. Manchester cried, affronted.

"I think maybe you should go and tie up your dog," Kate told her nephew.

He nodded his agreement and disappeared.

When the boy returned, he and Kate went outside and got into another taxi. They rode to the Quay, which was down near the Sydney Opera House, and boarded a ferry that took them across the harbor to the world-famous zoo.

They spent a happy morning examining one creature after another. Some were indigenous to Australia, while others might have been seen in any zoo.

Kate took a picture of Gil holding a baby koala. The little animal crunched nonchalantly on eucalyptus leaves all the while, willing to tolerate the idiosyncrasies of human beings.

When midday came, Kate and Gil had hot dogs and sodas for lunch. Kate reflected that her diet was going to hell on greased tracks; she'd have to get herself back on healthy food soon.

By early afternoon Gil was getting tired, so they took the ferry back to Sydney proper, found a movie house and bought tickets. Kate was glad to sit down, and she didn't really care what the show might be.

It was an action-adventure story, as it turned out, and both Gil and Kate were soon drawn into the plot, as much a part of things as the main character. When they came out two hours later, they were blinking in an effort to focus their eyes.

A quick check of her pocketbook showed that Kate was nearly out of money. "Let's go back to the hotel for a few minutes," she said to her nephew. "Then we'll have supper somewhere."

"Great," Gil agreed. It was an expression he'd heard in the movie, and he seemed pleased with himself for picking it up.

The hotel was several blocks away, but it felt good to walk after sitting for a couple of hours, and Kate and Gil played their game of exchanging idioms again as they went.

When they reached Kate's room, she opened one suitcase, and then another, and then another, searching for her traveler's checks. She finally found them in her overnight case, which was sitting in the bathroom on the counter.

A knock at the door brought her out, smiling and curious, her traveler's checks in one hand. The room looked as though it had been ransacked, she thought, as she passed by the trail of open suitcases she'd left behind her.

Sean was standing in the hallway when she opened the door, and she was so surprised that she just stood there for a moment, staring at him.

"When I go to America," Gil was saying cheerfully in the background, "I'm going to spend a whole month at Disneyland."

There was a slight change in Sean's expression, but his words sounded normal enough. "Aren't you going to kiss me, sheila?"

Kate realized that he was really there, and not a product of her overworked imagination, and she hurled her arms around his neck. "You're back early."

He removed her arms gently. "Surprised?" he asked, backing her into the room.

"Dad!" Gil shouted, hurling himself at his father. "We went to the zoo and saw a movie and once we had supper at McDonald's!"

"Good," Sean said quietly, ruffling Gil's hair with one hand. He was smiling, but there was something odd in his face as he looked around the room at Kate's suitcases.

Kate felt uneasy without knowing why. "Lucky we came back to get some money," she said to Sean. "If we hadn't, we would have missed you."

Sean was still looking at the suitcases, and it seemed to Kate that he was a little pale beneath his suntan. "Is that so?" he asked.

Kate wanted to shake him. "What's wrong?" she asked, keeping her voice as even as she could.

Sean wouldn't look at her. Instead, he turned his gaze toward Gil, who still stood at his side, looking up. "So, you're planning a trip to America, are you?" he asked.

Dread went through Kate like a cold wind when she realized the conclusion Sean was drawing from the rifled suitcases and his son's comment about Disneyland. "You don't understand," she said lamely.

"I think I do," Sean said, and his voice was like dry ice.

Gil chose that moment to whip his passport out of his jacket pocket and present it. "I could go anytime I wanted," he said proudly.

"I want you to wait for me by the elevators," Sean told his son, speaking in a voice that was all the more ominous for its quiet, measured tones.

Disappointment flashed in Gil's upturned face. "But we were going to have supper—"

"Go," Sean said flatly.

After casting one baffled, injured look in Kate's direction, Gil obediently walked out of the room and down the hallway. Kate would have gone after him, but Sean closed the door and barred her way.

"Pretty damned clever," he said.

Kate let out a furious sigh. "I wasn't planning to take your son away," she told him, shoving one hand through her hair.

Sean looked at her with contempt, but behind that she saw the pain of betrayal. "I was a fool to trust you. All of it—the talk, the lovemaking—you did it all to get into my good graces, so I'd leave you alone with Gil!"

"That's not true!" Kate cried. "You're deliberately misunderstanding the situation. Gil and I went to the zoo and then to the movies, and I was out of money, so I came back here to get my traveler's checks—that's why the suitcases look the way they do."

Sean didn't seem to hear her. He was like a geyser about to spew dangerous steam, and Kate had a terrible feeling that nothing she could say or do would move him. "Why did he have his passport, then?" he hissed, moving to grab Kate and then stopping himself at the last second. "Why was he talking about going to Disneyland?"

"I don't know why he brought his passport," Kate answered. "He got it out earlier to show it to me, and he probably just stuck it in his pocket."

"Why were you interested?" Sean demanded.

It was no use, and Kate knew it. "We did talk about going to America," she confessed. "But it was a someday kind of thing—not something immediate.''

''You're just like your father,'' Sean accused. ''You'll do anything, step on anybody, to get what you want!''

''No,'' Kate argued, her eyes filling with tears as she shook her head.

She might not have spoken at all for all Sean seemed to care. ''You're like her, too—why didn't I see that you're no better than she was?''

Kate couldn't bear any more. She grabbed Sean by the lapels of his windbreaker and shouted, ''Listen to me, damn you. I'm not my father, and I'm not Abby—I'm just Kate! And I'd die before I'd betray you, Sean Harris, because I love you more than I've ever loved anything or anybody!''

With a gentle kind of cruelty, Sean brushed Kate's hands away, turned on his heel and walked out, leaving the door open behind him.

Kate stepped into the hallway, her face wet with tears. ''Sean, please . . .'' she called after him, desperate.

''Goodbye,'' he said coldly without even turning around to look at her.

Kate sagged against the doorframe, closing her eyes as she heard the sound of an elevator bell. When it chimed again moments later, she knew Sean and Gil were gone.

She went back into her room, like something wounded, and, after closing and locking the door, she sprawled across the bed, too sickened to think or move. It was a long time before she gathered the strength to call the airport.

There was a flight leaving for Los Angeles in two hours. Numb from the core of her soul out, Kate booked a reservation on that flight, re-folded everything in her suitcases and called the desk for a bellhop. While she was waiting, she dialed Sean's number.

Fortunately Mrs. Manchester was the one to answer.

"This is Kate," the caller said brokenly. "May I please speak to Gil?"

The housekeeper sounded bewildered and kindly. "He's right here, Miss Blake," she said.

Gil came on the line a moment later. "Are you going, Aunt Kate?" he asked.

New tears welled in Kate's eyes. "I have to, sweetheart," she said. "You understand, don't you?"

Gil was silent for a long time, then he answered, "I guess I won't get to see Disneyland."

Kate dried her cheeks with the back of one hand. "Maybe another time," she said with forced cheerfulness. "I want you to promise to write to me, Gil, and tell me all about school and soccer and Snidely. Okay?"

"Okay," he replied.

"I love you, darling."

"And I love you, Aunt Kate," the little boy responded bravely.

Kate swallowed. "G-goodbye, Gil."

"Goodbye," came the forlorn reply.

Just as Kate was hanging up the telephone, a knock sounded at the door. The bellhop entered at her hoarse call of, "Come in!"

The young man loaded Kate's bags onto a luggage cart and started off toward the elevator. After a few moments spent struggling for composure, she followed.

All the way down to the desk and all the way to the airport, Kate kept hoping that Sean would show up. She had the scenario all worked out in her mind. He would say he was sorry, that he knew she would never do anything to hurt or betray him, and then they'd kiss and everything would be all right again.

Only it didn't happen that way.

There was no sign of Sean at the airport.

Kate had her passport checked and boarded the plane. Her last fantasy died when the doors of the craft were slammed shut. Sean wasn't going to come down the aisle and collect her and take her home.

She didn't have a home anymore.

Kate curled up in her seat, a bundle of despair and confusion, and stared out the window, watching the city of Sydney recede. She was really leaving—the dream was over.

After a while Kate slept. It was a fitful rest, and she awakened with a violent start when she felt someone's hand on her shoulder. Sean. Somehow, someway, he'd come for her. Maybe he'd been in the cockpit of the airplane all the time....

But it was only a blond flight attendant, smiling apologetically down at Kate. "I'm sorry, miss," she said, "but we're about to land in Auckland. You'll have to fasten your seat belt."

Kate sat up grumpily and fixed the belt. Maybe she'd get off in New Zealand, take a couple of days to compose herself and then go back and talk to Sean again. By now he had to be sorry for what he'd thrown away so thoughtlessly.

But even before the plane touched down, Kate had decided to go on to the States.

She'd done enough compromising. If Sean Harris wanted to talk to her, he was going to have to make the next move.

11

The child flung himself at Sean in a rage of pain and disbelief. "I hate you, I hate you!" he screamed, hammering at his father's chest with knotted fists. "You made her go away!"

Mrs. Manchester, who had inadvertently witnessed the scene, hurried off to another part of the house—but not before giving Sean a look that said her thoughts on the matter were similar to Gil's.

Feeling as though he were being torn in two, Sean grasped his son by the wrists to stop the attack. Then he knelt down on the floor of the entryway to look into his son's eyes. "Listen to me," he said hoarsely. "Please."

Gil still looked miserable, but he gave up the struggle. "Kate wasn't going to take me away," he insisted. "We were just going to have supper at a restaurant."

Sean gave a heavy sigh. "I know that now," he confessed. "And I'm sorry."

Gil's lower lip trembled and tears glistened in his eyes. "What good does being sorry do?" he challenged. "Aunt Kate's gone, and she'll probably never come back."

Kate was gone all right. While Sean had been agonizing over the fact that he'd been a fool not to trust her after all she'd been to him, she'd checked out of her hotel room, taken a cab to the airport and gotten on board a plane. By now she was probably halfway to New Zealand.

Sean rose to his feet. He was hurt and he was remorseful, but he wasn't really surprised. Kate had only done what he'd expected her to do all along—she had run back to Daddy when the first misunderstanding arose. Sean sighed, ruffled his son's hair and walked away.

"You could go and get her," Gil called after him in hopeful despair. "You could tell her you're sorry and bring her back."

Sean closed his eyes against his son's pain and his own. In time the hollows and canyons Kate's passing had left in their lives would fill in. All they needed was time.

"It's better this way," he answered, and kept walking.

The first thing Kate did when she reached home was take a long, hot shower. When that was done, she slept for thirty-six hours.

She opened her eyes to a world without Sean and Gil, and cried all the while she bathed and dressed and set out for the supermarket to buy food. She had no appetite at all, but her refrigerator was empty, and she knew she would eventually have to eat.

She encountered Brad in the yuppie section, where the miniature corn cobs and pickled crab apples were sold. He smiled and introduced the woman beside him.

"Allison, meet Kate Blake. Kate, my wife, Allison." He said "my wife" with a spiteful little twist, as though he expected Kate to fling herself down at his feet in despair.

"Allison," Kate acknowledged, properly shaking the hand of Brad's new bride. She was obviously a career woman—she wore a classic suit and there was a briefcase in the shopping cart, with the initials ABW engraved on the brass trim.

The brown-eyed, attractive blonde nodded, reserve evident in every supple line of her body. "Kate," she confirmed.

Kate excused herself and went wheeling off toward the produce section, hoping Brad had given up the life of crime once and for all, for his own sake as well as Allison's.

When Kate arrived home, loaded down with shopping bags, the doorman helped her carry them into her apartment. She was just handing him a tip when the telephone rang.

Until that morning Kate had kept it unplugged, and she wished now that she'd left it that way. She wasn't ready for a round with the senator or her mother.

The caller was Irene Blake. "Welcome back, darling."

Kate sighed. "Hello, Mother."

The doorman waved and slipped out, closing the door behind him.

"I can't tell you how glad your father and I are that you've finally come to your senses. I'm certainly disappointed, though, that you didn't bring Gil back with you."

"Hold on a moment, please," Kate said politely. Then she laid down the receiver, walked into the kitchen and took two aspirin from the bottle she kept in the cabinet by the stove. After washing them down with water, she went back to the telephone.

"I guess I'm not surprised that Sean wouldn't give an inch where the boy is concerned," Irene went on, and Kate wondered if her mother had been talking the whole time she was in the kitchen. "Australian men are notoriously stubborn, you know."

"And American men aren't?" Kate retorted, singularly annoyed.

"Your father is going to be stunned when he learns you didn't bring Gil home with you," Irene continued. "It's little enough to ask, I should think—"

"Mother," Kate interrupted with terse politeness. "I couldn't just grab the child and carry him off. That would be a crime."

"I'll tell you what is criminal, Katherine Blake—"

"Please don't," Kate broke in.

Irene took a sharp breath. "What's happened to you?" she demanded. "You're different."

"I'm older and wiser," Kate replied with a sigh.

"When are you joining your father in Washington?" Her mother pressed on.

"I'm not. He disinherited me, remember?"

"The senator didn't mean a thing by that, and you know it."

"He could have fooled me," Kate said.

"You're deliberately being difficult!"

Kate bit her lower lip. "I don't mean to be, Mother." She let out her breath in a rush. "Maybe we should talk later. We don't seem to be getting anywhere."

"All right," Irene agreed stiffly, "but I wish you were the kind of daughter we could depend on."

And I wish you were the kind of mother I could call "Mom," Kate thought. *I wish I could cry on your shoulder and tell you how much I'm hurting right now.* "Goodbye, Mother," she said.

The following Monday morning Kate returned to college. Although she had a degree, she wanted to teach in elementary school, and that required a few credits she didn't have.

Soon, her life became a lonely round of going to class, studying, sleeping and eating. When she was at home, she invariably wore her bathrobe.

"You know," her friend Maddie Phillips remarked one night as she sat filing her nails and watching Kate watch a rerun of *The Donna Reed Show*, "you're going to seed. Look at you—you've got all the personality of a doorstop."

Kate gave the glamorous redhead a look meant to be quelling. "Gee, thanks, Maddie. I admire you, too."

Maddie shook her nail file at Kate. She owned a small travel agency and lived one floor down in a two-bedroom with a terrace. *"And,"* she rushed on, as though her friend hadn't spoken, "you're getting fat in the bargain."

Kate picked up the remote control for the TV set and pushed the volume button until Maddie's voice was drowned out completely. Never one to be ignored, Maddie scrambled out of her chair and plopped down beside Kate on the couch. She wrenched the control from her hands and turned off the TV.

"The trouble with you, Kate Blake, is that you're in denial."

Kate glared at her. "You've been reading too much pop psychology," she said. "I'm not denying anything."

"Oh, no? I'll bet you've put on ten pounds in the past month—true?"

Kate sighed. "True," she admitted.

"And you're not sleeping very well, either," Maddie went on.

There were shadows under Kate's eyes, and she knew it. "Can't deny that," she said.

Impulsively, for Maddie was nothing if not impulsive, she took Kate's hand in hers. "What happened down there in Australia?" she asked. "It's time you told somebody."

Kate felt tears pressing behind her eyes. She'd been back for six weeks, and there hadn't been a word from Sean—not a letter or a telephone call. Apparently he still believed Kate had planned to kidnap his son.

"I fell in love," she said, and then the whole story spilled out of her. She told Maddie everything, except for the intimate details.

"That's so romantic," Maddie murmured when the tale ended.

"Romantic? I love that man and he hates me, Maddie. What's romantic about that?"

Maddie ignored the question. "You've got to go back there. Or at least write to him."

Kate folded her arms. "Not on your life," she said stubbornly. "Sean's the one who's in the wrong, not me."

"Hell of a comfort that will be when the baby comes," Maddie said shrewdly.

Kate's gaze shot to her friend's face. She hadn't consciously considered the possibility that she might be pregnant, but now she was forced to. And she knew all the signs were there; she'd just been ignoring them.

Maddie folded her arms and nodded sagely. "Denial," she said.

"Oh, God," Kate replied, and she began to cry.

Maddie slipped an arm around Kate's shoulders. "Sean has a right to know," she said softly.

Kate shook her head. If Sean knew about the baby, there would be all sorts of problems. Hadn't he said he wouldn't have his children living on separate continents? No, it was better if he never learned he'd fathered another child.

"You're not being fair," Maddie insisted.

"Was it fair of Sean to accuse me of trying to steal his son?" Kate paused to sniffle. "He claimed to love me, Maddie, and yet he wouldn't even let me explain.''

''There must have been a reason.''

Kate sighed, remembering the kidnapping attempt against Gil, the one Sean had blamed on the senator. She had to admit, to herself at least, that he had more cause to worry than the average parent. ''Maybe,'' she said grudgingly.

Maddie gathered up her purse and handed the TV control back to Kate. ''Here. Watch reruns till your eyes cross,'' she told her friend. ''See if I care.''

Kate looked up at Maddie. ''You do care,'' she said. ''Thank you for that.''

Maddie smiled sadly, touched Kate's shoulder, then left. Kate switched off the TV, crawled into bed and cried.

The next morning, a Saturday, her father returned from Washington and summoned her to his study in the fancy house on the hill. Because she had no classes that day, Kate put on her roomiest pair of jeans and a loose T-shirt and drove up there.

Her mother met her at the front door, elbowing aside a uniformed maid to do so. ''Look at you,'' she said, running her eyes over Kate with an expression of horror. ''You're a wreck!''

"You don't know the half of it, Mother," Kate replied, stepping past Irene to enter the house. "What does Daddy want?"

Irene made a face as she closed the door. "You needn't sound so cynical, Katherine. Your father is merely trying to bridge the gap between you, and it's more of an effort than *you've* made, I dare say."

Kate followed her mother down the hallway and into the familiar study.

"I want you to go back to Australia and fetch my grandson," the senator said, the moment he and his daughter were alone in that room full of books and expensive leather furniture.

Kate bit her lower lip, then answered, "I can't do that."

"Nonsense," John Blake retorted. "You simply pick the boy up at school, then the two of you get on a plane and come home."

Kate groped for a chair and fell into it. She felt dizzy and just a bit sick to her stomach. "You're serious, aren't you?" she whispered, her eyes round.

"Of course I'm serious," the senator replied.

"Why do you want Gil so badly?"

"He's my flesh and blood, that's why. He's all I have left of my firstborn child."

Kate closed her eyes for a moment. The room seemed to be spinning around her. "It's really true," she marveled. "You *were* behind the kidnapping attempt."

"Harris forced me into that by denying me my grandchild...." the senator began.

Kate held up one hand in a plea for silence and eased herself out of her chair. "Please," she whispered. "I don't want to hear any more."

"Katherine!"

Kate stumbled out of the room, closed the door and leaned against it, as though to hold back something ugly.

After leaving her parents' house, she drove straight to the cemetery where Abby was buried, parked her car and made her way awkwardly over the slippery green grass to the family plot.

Abby's headstone was a giant angel, with a trumpet pressed to its lips. *Fitting,* Kate thought, kneeling nearby. "I thought you were so wonderful," she said sadly. "Know what, Abby? It hurts to find out you were only human."

A light breeze blew through the sunny graveyard, ruffling Kate's hair. She ran her hand gently over the place where her only sister lay. "I'm going to have Sean's baby," she went on. "I don't expect you or anyone else in the family to understand, but I had to tell someone."

Kate paused, looking up at the blue, blue sky with its lacy white clouds. "I'll never understand why you didn't want Sean, Abby. He's so wonderful—"

It seemed that Abby challenged her then, although Kate knew the exchange was happening only inside her own head. *If he's so wonderful, why did you leave him?*

Kate bit down on her lower lip, her eyes on the ground. "I know now that I shouldn't have," she answered softly. "It was all a misunderstanding—we could have talked it out."

Give it up. You're Daddy's little girl and you always were. You wouldn't have been happy anywhere but right here in Seattle.

"That's not true," Kate argued. "I was happy in Australia. Happier than I've ever been."

Then go back. You have my blessing.

Kate shook her head. "I haven't the courage," she said.

Why not?

"I've been so wrong about everybody in my life—you, Brad, Daddy. The one time when I was right, I didn't stay and fight—I ran away like a coward. I'm afraid of doing that again."

After a long time, she rose, touched the face of the trumpeting angel and whispered, "Goodbye, Abby."

*   *   *

Sean nodded and left the cockpit. The passengers were still trailing out, and he had to struggle to keep himself from hurrying them along.

At last he was able to escape. His suitcase in one hand, Sean strode along the walkway and left the terminal. It was a chilly September day—down under it would be spring. Here it was the fall of the year, and the leaves were beginning to turn.

Sean shook his head. This part of the world was a strange place, whether the Yanks liked to admit it or not.

He got a cab right away, but he had to repeat the address twice before the driver understood. Sean grinned to himself. Everybody here had an accent—it was no wonder they didn't comprehend plain English.

Kate's glasses were riding on the tip of her nose as she read from her algebra textbook and got her prenatal vitamins down from the shelf at the same time. Without looking away from the book, she dumped a capsule onto the counter, lifted it to her mouth and swallowed it. She nearly choked and was gulping down water when the doorbell rang.

Muttering, she meandered into the living room. It was probably the Henderson kids sell-ing candy or calendars so some team they were on could buy new uniforms.

When she opened the door, however, Sean was standing there, looking like an ad for flight school in his spiffy blue uniform. He took off his hat in a shy gesture and said, "Hello, Kate."

Kate's throat constricted around the prenatal vitamin capsule. "Hello," she managed, taking off her glasses.

Sean grinned slightly, bringing on a poignant pain in the region of Kate's heart. "May I come in?"

She stepped back, her glasses in one hand and her algebra book in the other. "Sure," she said, long after the fact.

Sean set his hat on a table. He had a bag, too, and he put that on the floor at his feet. "I was wrong," he said, just like that.

Kate stared at him. Even if she could have spoken, she wouldn't have known what to say.

He looked at Kate for a moment with his heart in his eyes, and then he went to the windows and stood with his back to her, gazing out at the city. "I'm living in San Francisco now," he told her.

At last Kate found her voice. "You're still with Austra-Air?"

Without turning around, Sean nodded. "Yes. So Gil and I are giving the States a chance to win us over."

Kate's heart was beating faster than it had since she'd returned from Australia. "Take him to Disneyland," she suggested softly. "That'll cinch it for you."

Now Sean turned. "I'm sorry, Kate," he said, meeting her eyes. "I should have trusted you."

"You're right," Kate said. "You should have."

"Will you give me a second chance?"

Kate had prayed to hear those words, but she hadn't really expected an answer. For that reason, she hadn't rehearsed a reply, and she just stood there, stricken.

Sean came closer, laying his hands gently on her shoulders. "Kate?" His voice was low and hoarse. "I'm ready to make some compromises, to prove I love you enough to make this thing work."

Kate swallowed. "Like what?" she managed.

"Like living in San Francisco. Like letting you adopt Gil if you want."

Kate was so moved that her voice came out sounding strangled and squeaky. "You'd do that? You'd make him legally my child?"

Sean nodded. "I would," he affirmed.

Tears welled in Kate's eyes—happy tears. Her arms went automatically around his neck. "What's my part of this bargain?" she asked with a half smile.

He chuckled. "Ah, sheila, I'm glad you asked that," he answered, slipping his arms around her thickening waist. "Come closer and I'll show you."

"I want a proposal first," Kate protested primly.

Sean laughed. "All right, then," he agreed. "Will you marry me, Kate Blake? Will you share my life and my bed? Will you be a mother to my son?"

"I will," Kate vowed, raising one hand to prove the oath.

That was when Sean kissed her. At first it was a gentle, tentative kiss, but then she felt his body harden into a familiar readiness. His tongue plundered the depths of her mouth, and Kate's knees turned to mashed potatoes.

When he lifted her into his arms without breaking the kiss, she didn't demur. She wanted whatever he had to give her.

"There is one little thing I should mention," she said breathlessly when they reached the bedroom and Sean was lifting her sweatshirt off over her head.

He bent and kissed the rounded tops of each of her breasts. "What?" he asked.

Kate drew in a sharp breath as he unfastened her bra and quickly tossed it aside. "You're probably going to be mad," she warned.

Sean lifted her, so that she was forced to wrap her legs around his waist. That put her breasts at mouth level, and he took immediate advantage of the situation. "I'll get over it fast," he assured her between suckles.

Kate was moaning. "Maybe I should—oh, God—wait."

Sean turned to her other breast. "Tell me," he said.

"I'm pregnant," Kate blurted out.

He eased her slowly, gently to the bed, bending over her. "Damnedest thing," he murmured, shaking his head. "I could have sworn you just said you were pregnant."

"I did, and I am. That is, *we* did and I am."

Sean laughed, and the tears glistening in his eyes were a touching contrast. "My God, sheila—that's wonderful."

Kate drew him down toward her lips and her body. Both were his to claim. "I'm very glad you think so, Captain Harris," she said, and then she kissed him, unbuttoning his shirt at the same time.

The warm, hairy hardness of his chest felt good under her palms. She squirmed as he unfastened and unzipped her jeans.

"I thought you were a little chubby," he remarked when the kiss had ended. His lips were against her bare belly then, and Kate was trembling in anticipation.

"Thanks a lot," she muttered.

He laughed again. "As soon as you've gotten over having this one," he said, moving lower. "We'll start another."

Kate was already writhing slightly, for he was very near his destination. She felt the downy curtain part and she moaned. After that, all her words were incoherent.

Once the first shattering pinnacle had been reached, Kate lay gasping on the bed, watching Sean as he removed the rest of his clothes. When he was naked, he stretched out over her on the bed.

"I thought I'd die for missing you," he said hoarsely, and his eyes glinted in the half-darkness of the bedroom.

Kate ran her hands along his magnificent back. She didn't speak, for her body told him everything.

With a groan, Sean entered her, murmuring words of love and need as he completed that first long, delicious stroke.

Kate welcomed him in the way that women have received their men since time immemorial. She thrust her hips upward to draw him into her very depths.

"You'll make a madman of me yet," he moaned, withdrawing slowly and then gliding into her again.

Fire had been ignited inside Kate, and the flames were rising higher and higher. She whimpered as her temperature climbed, and hurled herself at Sean in a wanton search for what only he could give her.

"That's it," he whispered, tucking his hands under her bottom to urge her on. "That's it, Katie-did—I want everything."

She was soaring toward a molten sky, borne high on tongues of fire. "Sean—Sean—"

He buried his face in her neck even as he buried his manhood in her depths. His strokes were the fierce lunges of a conqueror, and Kate's surrender was complete.

With a cry of jubilation, she exploded like a nova, and Sean was only moments behind her.

When it was over, they lay still. For Kate, Sean's rapid heartbeat and ragged breathing were music. She'd thought she'd never hold him like this again, never feel the unique planes and hollows of his body fitted to hers.

"The least you can do," she said when she was capable, "is buy me dinner."

Sean gave her a playful swat. "Buy you dinner, is it? I ought to turn you over my knee for not telling me about the baby sooner."

"I've only known about it for a few weeks myself," Kate defended. "Shall we send out for Chinese or walk down to the corner for fish and chips?"

"I'm not walking anywhere," Sean said. He'd slid down to her breast and was rolling his tongue around her nipple. "Besides, chow mein isn't what I'm hungry for."

Kate shifted slightly to give him better access. "We deliver," she said.

Later, when the loving was over, she told him about her estrangement with her father and her decision to become an elementary school teacher.

Sean thought teaching was a grand idea, since Kate liked kids so much, but he surprised her where the rift with her father was concerned. He said she should try to make things right, or she might come to regret it someday.

12

The senator stepped uneasily through the front door of the gracious home overlooking San Francisco Bay. He held his hat in one hand and clutched the front of his overcoat closed as though he expected someone to snatch it away. Beside him, Irene slipped out of her snow-dusted mink coat and gave Kate a cautious kiss on the cheek.

"You look wonderful, darling," she said.

"Are you my grandparents?" Gil asked forthrightly.

Irene was crying, and the senator looked at the little boy with a helpless expression Kate had never seen on his face before.

"Yes," Sean said quietly when no one spoke. "These are your grandparents." He stood behind Gil, one hand resting on the boy's shoulder.

The senator's weary blue eyes moved from

Kate's face to Sean's. "I apologize for everything," he said.

Sean nodded without speaking, took Kate's hand and led her out of the room.

"I wish I didn't have to leave for Honolulu tonight," he said, drawing her as close as he could, given her bulging stomach.

She laughed and laid both her hands on his cheeks. "Oh, you poor man," she teased.

Sean's hand rested on the rounded sides of Kate's stomach. "You'll take very good care of my daughter, won't you?"

"The best," Kate assured him.

He kissed her, and Kate was sorry he was going away. If they'd been alone, she might have taken him by the hand and led him up the stairs to their spacious bedroom.

"Keep that up and I'll have my way with you right here, Captain Harris," she said in a conversely prim voice.

He laughed and squeezed her bottom. "I'm shocked, Mrs. Harris," he scolded. "What would the PTA think if they heard their vice president carrying on like this?"

Kate shrugged. "Kiss me again," she said.

Sean obliged graciously.

When he'd left for the airport, Kate went back to the living room. Her mother was sitting in a chair next to the fireplace, watching fondly as Gil

and the senator plundered the brightly wrapped
gifts under the Christmas tree.

"No fair shaking," Kate protested.

The old man and the boy looked at her with
similar smiles.

"Can I give Grandpa his present now, Mom?"
Gil asked.

"No," Kate answered, settling into her favorite chair and spreading the colorful afghan she
was knitting over her knees. "Christmas is still
three days away."

"Scrooge," complained the senator.

"Please?" Gil wheedled.

Kate caved in. After all, it was Christmas and
she was no disciplinarian, anyway. "All right,
but just one," she conceded.

"Our gifts are arriving later," the senator
confided to his daughter as Gil ran up the stairs
to fetch the special set of Australian stamps he'd
set aside for his grandfather.

"By boxcar," confirmed Irene.

Kate chuckled and tended to her knitting.

The snow had stopped in the early morning,
two days later, when Sean crawled into bed beside her and drew her into his arms.

"Hello, Mrs. Harris," he said, his lips moving against her temple.

"Exactly who are you?" Kate retorted, yawning. But she snuggled closer.

He placed a warm hand on her stomach. "Very funny," he said. "Did you lay down the law to the senator, by the way?"

"Uh-huh," Kate said. "He won't be bothering me about coming back to work for him after this. I told him that being vice president of the PTA at Gil's school is the closest I'm ever going to get to politics."

"How did he react?" Sean asked, stretching and making himself comfortable beside Kate.

She giggled at the picture that came to her mind. "He blustered, but I wasn't intimidated. After all, he was wearing Gil's Mickey Mouse ears at the time."

Sean laughed and stretched again. "I'm going to sleep," he announced.

"No, you're not," Kate replied.

BARBARA BRETTON

Destiny's Child

Dakota Wylie was a typical twentieth-century woman
living a typical twentieth-century life—chaotic! But it
was calmer than the existence she found herself leading
in eighteenth-century New Jersey with Patrick Devane.
He was stubborn and cynical and thought her brazen and
unladylike. But there was no denying the passion
between them. Caught in a time of tumultuous change,
Dakota and Patrick found their hearts on fire with hate
as well as love. Now Patrick was accused of spying. And
Dakota had to decide whether she had traveled two
hundred years through time to lie with a man who was
now branded an enemy....

Don't miss *Destiny's Child* this September, at your
favorite retail outlet.